YOURS FOREVER

LANTERN BAY, BOOK 5

SOPHIE HAYDON

BAY BOOKS

Yours Forever
by Sophie Haydon

—The Mackenzies—
A Place Called Home
Secrets at Parata Bay
Escape to Shelter Springs
What you See in the Stars
Second Chance at Whisper Creek
Summer at the Lakehouse Café

—Lantern Bay—
Yours to Give
Yours to Treasure
Yours to Cherish
Yours to Keep
Yours Forever
Yours to Love

For more information about this author, visit:
https://sophiehaydon.com

© 2022 Sophie Haydon
ISBN 978-1-99-102111-3 (epub)
ISBN 978-1-99-102112-0 (2022 Amazon Print Edn)
ISBN 978-1-99-102134-2 (2022 Draft2Digital Print Edn)

CONTENTS

Prologue   1
Chapter 1   8
Chapter 2   23
Chapter 3   41
Chapter 4   54
Chapter 5   72
Chapter 6   87
Chapter 7   102
Chapter 8   116
Chapter 9   131
Chapter 10   145
Chapter 11   162
Chapter 12   176
Epilogue   188

Afterword   193
Yours to Love   195
Also by Sophie Haydon   197

Let your heart guide you like a lantern in the dark
— **Dan Millman**

PROLOGUE

The front doorbell rang out the chimes of Big Ben, stopping abruptly before the last note. Flo winced. The chime, like just about everything else in her house, was faulty. She just hoped the woman who'd rung the bell didn't notice. Flo had a lot riding on this meeting.

She smoothed down the white linen shirt she'd worn for the occasion, but it sprang back up into the folds it had assumed while she'd sat at her desk, going over her accounts one more time. Unfortunately, it didn't make any difference how many times she went over the profit-and-loss statement her friend, Maddy, had prepared for her, the bottom line didn't change. It was still in the red.

Taking a deep breath and fixing a smile on her face, Flo walked briskly down the grand hallway to the front door and swung it open. Charlotte Kincaid stood there—the town's new lawyer, councillor and chairperson of the Festival of Lights committee—a picture of the kind of cool glamour which was alien to Flo.

"Flo," greeted Charlotte, her glossy red lips turning up into a warm smile, which made Flo's heart sink even further.

She hated the fact she couldn't even dislike this powerful woman who had it all.

"Hello, Charlotte," said Flo, standing aside to allow her to step into the hall. "I'm glad you could make it before the weather turned." She glanced into her front garden, where the buds of spring and tender shoots wouldn't be nurtured by the weather forecast over the next few days.

"Your garden is looking as beautiful as ever. It's been a real drawing card for our committee."

Flo looked at her sharply. "Not the only one I hope," she said, her smile fading. She didn't like the sound of the past tense. "Please, come on through to the meeting room."

Flo tried to close the door quietly, but the stained glass in the windows rattled as usual in their lead frames. They were on the list to fix, but not high enough to have done anything about them yet.

Flo opened the door to the meeting room, which was the jewel in the house's crown. The size of two rooms, with dual-aspect windows, one of which opened up onto the lauded gardens, it still retained a sense of its old grandeur. Flo liked to think that what it lacked in sleek, modern features, it made up for in character. But Charlotte remained in the hall.

"Well," said Flo, making sure she kept her smile on her face. "I was surprised to hear from you. Did you want to make some special arrangements for the next monthly meeting? Would you like me to cater for someone's birthday, like I did…" She trailed off as Charlotte shook her head decisively and held up her hand. She did it with her trademark grace and warmth, but even so it was clear who was in charge of this conversation. And it wasn't Flo. "Like I did last year?" finished Flo, in a small voice.

"No, that won't be necessary, thank you."

Butterflies danced in Flo's stomach—and not the good kind. The angry, dementor-like creatures which presaged

2

nothing good. "Oh. How about a cup of tea and cake? I'm baking some cakes for the café and have just got one out of the oven." She took a deep, exaggerated sniff of the air, which was redolent with freshly baked apple cake, knowing she was going over the top but unable to stop herself. She never got nervous, but she was now. The income which the committee brought in meant the difference between keeping her business afloat and it sinking.

"Not if they're destined for Amber's café. I wouldn't want to cut into your cash flow."

"I assure you, you're not. The apple cake is for my guests. I've a house full at the moment and I've a feeling the place would empty pretty quickly if I stopped baking." She widened her smile and opened the kitchen door for Charlotte to enter.

"It's good to know your business is going well."

Is it? thought Flo to herself. Why? But there was no way Flo was going to invite the sort of answer she half-expected, so, instead, she went ahead into the kitchen and hoped like hell that Charlotte would follow her.

When she heard Charlotte sigh in defeat, Flo let out a deeply held breath of relief, and went to cut the cake, which was placed on a cooling tray on the scrubbed pine table at the center of the room. The cakes destined for Amber's café were stacked up in boxes, ready to deliver later. Charlotte glanced at them.

"I thought Amber had her own chef on the premises."

"She does. But I guess she likes my cakes, too."

Flo turned away, not wanting to see Charlotte's look of pity. She knew Amber appreciated her cakes, but she also knew that her best friend was doing her a big favor by sending work her way whenever she could.

Flo began cutting two large slices, shifting the knife to make them even more generous—she felt in sudden need of comfort—but stopped when Charlotte placed one manicured hand on top of hers.

"Flo, I'm not stopping. This is merely a courtesy visit."

Flo froze and knew her mouth had dropped open—it felt dry with fear.

"I'm sorry to inform you the committee has decided that it can no longer meet in your dining room."

"The *meeting* room," corrected Flo, determined to give her domestic room a more business edge. "I call it the meeting room," she added for clarification. "We have always used it for meetings, ever since my grandparents' days, and probably before them. Forever, in fact. It's always been a real community hub." She nodded, willing Charlotte to agree.

But Charlotte's expression suggested the opposite of agreement. "It doesn't matter what you call it, it's still not suitable. It never was and certainly isn't now when we have no choice but to move into a digital future where some of our members will join us by computer. Face it, Flo, your Wi-Fi isn't reliable and we can't have a repeat of what happened last time."

Flo felt her lips tremble, and she pressed them together. She shrugged. "That was a one off," she said, her voice unusually faint. "I thought the table was secure."

"It was held up by a pile of books."

"If Trevor hadn't kicked the books, it would have been fine."

"But Trevor *did* kick the books, and it *wasn't* fine. His laptop was ruined when the water jug overturned on it."

"Didn't insurance cover it?"

"He had to use his own insurance policy because yours had lapsed. And he lost documents which hadn't been backed up."

"They should have been backed up," said Flo, repeating something Maddy—not only one of her best friends and her accountant but also a computer whizz—had once told her. It meant little to her.

"And *you* should have been insured. You weren't. I have to say that several of us wanted to move our meetings at that point, but Trevor refused, saying that we'd always held them here, even in your grandmother's time."

"But Trevor's gone now."

"Indeed. And I'm now the chairperson and am determined to move with the times. Which means, Flo, we will meet at the new community center in future. It has all the modern technical support we require."

"No!" Her heart raced, and she tugged at the neckline of her top. She felt as if she couldn't breathe. "I mean, I'll sort things out. I can put in technical stuff. What is it you want?"

Charlotte's face had changed from a professional frown to sympathy. Flo wasn't sure it was an improvement. "Computers, reliable Wi-Fi, data projection facilities."

Flo opened her mouth to speak, but nothing came out. She didn't even know what data projection facilities looked like. "But, but..." She dropped the knife, which was still hovering over the cake, with a clatter. Charlotte looked relieved that Flo no longer held a knife. "But it has photos of the committee hung around the wall. It has history. Doesn't that mean anything?"

"I'm sorry, Flo, our minds are made up."

Flo couldn't do anything but follow Charlotte out to the front door, which she rarely used. They stood under the sheltering porch as the rain stopped threatening and began to fall in earnest. It felt like a comment on her change in fortune.

Charlotte turned to her. "We didn't take this decision lightly, Flo. And I'm sorry, I know the income which came with it was useful to you."

More than useful, Flo thought. It was the difference

between surviving and not. She cleared her throat. "Don't worry about my income. I'm fine." She refused to grovel any more to Miss Perfect.

But it didn't look as if Miss Perfect believed her for one minute. "That's good. I'm afraid we have no choice. The dining room is simply past its best." She glanced at the peeling wallpaper in the hall, which mirrored the state of decoration everywhere in the house. Flo placed her hand over it, as if smoothing it up the wall would make it stick. It didn't. As soon as she moved her hand, the wallpaper re-formed into a drooping curl, as if even the walls were weeping.

"I have plans to change the wallpaper."

The woman touched Flo gently on the arm. "It's not only wallpaper we need. We simply can't run the committee properly without technical support. If you wouldn't stall on the contract I set up for you to fund your house improvements, this wouldn't be happening. The money is there. All you have to do is ask."

"I can't do that," said Flo through gritted teeth. "If I'd known who was funding the project, I'd never have signed it."

"But sign it you did."

All thoughts of pride went out the window. "Please, could you give me one more chance? I really want to do this on my own and the money I get from using my dining room for meetings is an important part of my income stream. Please." Flo wasn't above begging now.

A big drop of rain found its way through a rusting hole in the porch roof and plopped onto Charlotte's nose. She looked up, and the drops formed a continuous drip on her head until she shifted to one side. Flo's heart sank even further.

"Okay, Flo, you have until the Festival of Lights to get things right."

Flo nearly fell over in surprise. Anyone else and the rain coming through the roof would have been the last straw, but this was Charlotte Kincaid she was dealing with. For all Flo's willingness to dislike Miss Perfect—the woman who had it all—she knew Charlotte was also kind.

"Thank you! You won't regret it." Flo reached out to grab Charlotte's hands, possibly to kiss them, she couldn't have said, but Charlotte stepped away before any such embarrassing display of emotion could slip out.

"And after the festival, if things still aren't up to scratch, we'll have to find another venue. Goodbye, Flo."

Gloomily, Flo leaned against the doorjamb and watched Charlotte walk through the rain up the brick-paved path to the road.

Two months to get things right. If she didn't, she wouldn't have any funds to pay her rates. And, with the council surveyor's inspection looming, she might have to close. And, if she had to close, there would be no Flo's Place, no Backpacker's Lodge and no home for Flo, because she simply couldn't afford to live there without the house paying its way.

She'd come to the end of the road. She'd either have to close or agree to accept money from the one person in the world she wanted nothing to do with—the man who'd broken her heart ten years earlier.

---

1

*T*wenty-four hours later, Flo sat back on her haunches and looked around at the scraps of wallpaper which were all she had to show for hours of scraping away at the walls in her meeting room. Although much of the beautiful, flowered wallpaper had come away from the seams after twenty years of clinging to the walls, the rest had proved positively unwilling to leave its long-time home.

She was relieved to hear the latch on the garden gate clatter. It meant she could have a break. She got up, stretched, and went to the window. Despite the heavy rain which appeared to have settled in for the day, it was easy to identify the person running up the garden path. The brilliant red hair would have been clue enough that it was Amber, her other best friend. But the bright yellow raincoat with rainbow motif confirmed it, as did the sunny smile she shot at Flo through the window.

Flo went to the door to meet her. Amber just dodged the steady rivulet of rain which now streamed through the rusting holes on the porch roof.

"Why didn't you come round the back?"

"I couldn't reach the back door without getting my feet wet. Looks like the creek will overflow later. It's covering your path already." Amber shivered as some cold water found its way down the back of her coat. She looked up. "You should get this porch fixed."

"I should get a lot of things fixed," said Flo wearily, as she stood aside to let Amber in. Behind Amber, the lights, left over from Christmas eight months earlier, brightened the afternoon gloom. Flo glanced across her garden to the road along which only a few people walked in the rain. One of them was a middle-aged man who was looking directly at her. They stared at each other for a moment before he hurried on, disappearing round a corner. Flo frowned as she closed the door.

"Did someone bring you?" she asked Amber.

"No! David thinks I came by car, but you know how much I love walking in the rain." She shrugged off her coat and draped it onto a hook on the old-fashioned coat stand, so the drips would catch in the umbrella drip pan. She turned to Flo and gave her a big hug. "Now, let's see what we can do with your dining room."

"Meeting room," Flo mumbled. Maybe she'd give up on that.

She followed Amber down the impressive hallway, with its carved kauri pillars and archway, opened the door and switched on the lights. There was a fraction of a second delay between the moment she depressed the Bakelite switch and the lights turning on. The electrics were also on her 'to do' list.

"Apart from the kitchen, this is my favorite room in the house," said Flo, automatically drawn to the French windows which opened out onto the large front garden. She glanced out, but the street was empty, and the rain was falling heavier now.

"I love it, too, just as it is."

Flo sighed and turned to Amber. "Unfortunately, we're in the minority. Everyone else seems to want perfection." She adjusted one of the oil paintings which hung from the wooden picture rail that ran around the room. "They want electronics, rather than character; modern rather than old. I need help, Amber. I'm out of my depth here. I know what *I* like. Trouble is, no one else seems to like it." She smiled at her best friend. "Except you, that is."

"And I'm not sure I'm going to be of much help. Maybe you should ask Rachel or Lizzi what to do. They're far more sophisticated than me."

"Your sisters' tastes are unquestionable. But I need something which is still me, if you know what I mean."

Amber shot Flo one of her big smiles. "I know exactly what you mean. And I feel honored you should choose me to help you be you."

Flo smiled at the very Amber-like response but also felt a wobble of nerves. "But maybe no rainbows. Less of the hippy vibe and more of the welcoming, homely yet still historic vibe. No offense."

"None taken." Amber opened up the shopping bags she'd brought with her and withdrew some swatches and wallpaper books. "I was talking to David, as he deals in heritage buildings, and he gave me these to be going on with. I will temper my hippy vibe with his sophisticated, knowledgeable vibe."

Flo's nerves vanished instantly. "And that, my friend, sounds pretty perfect to me."

"I also brought this," said Amber, pulling a wallpaper steamer from yet another bag. "David says it'll make things easier. You know he'd happily come around after work and help you, too."

Flo looked away. "I know. But he's working with Rob and I don't want your brother involved. Anyway," she said, avoiding Amber's gaze. She really didn't want to talk with Amber about her big brother, Rob, again. "If you want to get the steamer going, I'll keep working with the scraper." She gave Amber a quick hug, as much to apologize for her comment about Rob as anything else. "Thank you so much. I really appreciate your help."

"It's no problem. You know I'd do anything for you. But I still wish—"

Flo stepped away and held up her hand. "No talk of your big brother, please. Let's just get on with this." She pushed a lock of hair, which had escaped her ponytail, behind her ear and scanned the walls. "We have a lot to do."

Flo picked up her scraper once more and pulled a long piece away from the wall, revealing yet another layer of wallpaper.

"Oh, my goodness!" said Amber, as Flo peeled away the second layer to reveal a third.

"I know. My ancestors certainly loved their wallpaper."

"And so do I," said Amber. "Once we get this lot off, we can replace it with a design from those books I brought."

Flo looked doubtfully at the wallpaper books Amber had brought with her. "They look expensive."

"Don't worry about that. David said he'd get you whatever you wanted."

"I can't accept that! It must cost a fortune."

"You won't be getting it for nothing! He knew you'd say that, and he especially asked for regular deliveries of your food. You know what my cooking's like."

Flo did, and she completely understood David's request.

"Consider it a deal."

They were soon busy peeling away wallpaper, with folk music providing a backdrop to the quiet scraping sounds and Amber's chatter. Flo found it a relief to get her teeth into something—something physical she could do while she tried to figure out how she could afford the technical things which Charlotte had requested. At least if the room looked good, she reasoned, she'd be more than halfway there. And this wouldn't cost her anything—only her and Amber's time.

It was Amber's silence which alerted Flo that something had happened. Amber's talk had been a soothing antidote to Flo's thoughts.

She looked across the room to see Amber had stopped working and was peering beneath a long strip of wallpaper.

"What's up?"

"I'm not sure," said Amber. "There seems to be something behind this wallpaper."

"A wall?"

"Very funny." Amber put down the steamer, took a metal scraper and tapped the edge against the wall. A sharp metallic sound rang out. Flo frowned and jumped up, joining Amber as she pulled off a long strip of wallpaper, revealing the edge of something which was lodged in the wall.

Flo ran her finger along the side and found some heavy-duty hinges. "That's weird. What on earth is it?"

"I don't know. But, whatever it is, it was placed here after the other layers of wallpaper, and before this last one."

"It was last wallpapered in the late 1990s, I think."

Flo peeled back the remaining layers and scraped around the object until it was clear. They both stood back. "It's a funny place to have a safe. Behind wallpaper." Flo gnawed her lip and frowned, completely puzzled by the find. "I didn't know we ever had a safe."

"It's *really* weird that it's been wallpapered over."

"Very weird."

"Who did the wallpapering?"

"It would have been Gran because I'm pretty sure it was done after Grandad died."

"So… if your Gran wallpapered over it, she knew it was there," said Amber.

"And she wanted it hidden," said Flo slowly, as she fingered the gunmetal gray surface, before resting her finger on the lock. There was no handle, only a lock. "Why on earth would she have wanted to do that?"

Amber shrugged. "I guess you'll only know for sure when you find out what's inside."

Sometimes Amber could surprise Flo by showing a display of flawless logic.

"You're right."

"I wonder where the key is."

"It would only be in one place."

"Not one of *the* key rings?"

Flo nodded. Her friends teased her about the old iron circular key rings, from which hung all shapes and sizes of keys, most of which looked as if they were over a hundred years old. They hung on a hook in the kitchen, just as they always had in her grandmother's time. "I don't know what locks half of them are for. But I haven't had the heart to ditch any, in case I ever discover a lock without a key."

"Like now."

"Like now."

For a moment they looked at each other and it wasn't excitement, but a sense of nervous tension which hung in the air between them.

"But what if it's something secret? Something which your Gran wanted to hide from everyone?"

The same thought had occurred to Flo. It made her feel queasy. What could her grandmother have possibly wanted to hide from the world? Whatever it was, it couldn't be good news. And she really didn't want to receive any more bad news. She was sick of bad news.

"I don't know," she whispered. Silence fell between them. Only the steady patter of rain on the window and the surge of waves pounding on the shore out the back of the house filled the silence.

Suddenly, there was a banging on the door. They both jumped, and Amber shrieked. Flo recovered first, shaking her head at how carried away she'd been by Amber's imagination and her own fears. "It's only the door."

Amber gave an uncertain laugh. "David's always saying I let my imagination run away with me." She shrugged nervously. "For a moment, I imagined it was an avenging angel or something."

"I'll face the avenging angel. Although why they didn't just enter, I don't know. Everyone else does." Except, she thought, going along the darkening hallway to the front door, Charlotte Kincaid. God, she hoped it wasn't her again. Perhaps Amber was on to something. Perhaps it *was* an avenging angel come to pay a visit.

Flo flung the door open and her thoughts were confirmed. It *was* an avenging angel, just a different one to the one she'd imagined. Outside, under the decrepit porch, stood Rob Connelly, someone she wanted to see even less than Charlotte.

"Rob!" she said, annoyed that despite her wish to avoid her ex-boyfriend, there was a note of excitement in her voice. She immediately tamped it down. "What are *you* doing here?" She was pleased she sounded annoyed.

"Good to see you, too, Flo," said Rob with his usual low

rumble. His voice had always got to her, its vibrations traveling deep inside of her, making a connection she no longer wanted. He was wearing a bushman's oiled jacket left open, with worn jeans and a black t-shirt underneath. He was broader, more muscled than he'd been when he'd left Flo and New Zealand all those years ago—a period of time which she thought of as forever. He was, not to put too fine a point on it, even more sexy than before.

Flo forced herself to ignore her instinctive reaction, which was to jump into his arms and allow him to carry her off. She'd done that years ago and look how that had ended. She couldn't even allow herself to give her usual warm welcome to visitors, because Rob was different. Rob was the man who'd hurt her beyond pain itself.

"I guess you're here to see your little sister?" One thing was certain, Rob wouldn't have come to see Flo. When they'd last met, she'd made it clear she wanted nothing to do with him.

"Yep. Mind if I come in?" He glanced up at the leaking roof through which rain now ran in thick, rope-like cords. "I would have come to the back door as usual, but the path by the beach is impassable now. You really should—"

"Get that seen to," she interrupted. "I know, and I will."

Flo opened the door wide, and he stepped into the hallway. She suddenly remembered how he used to call and see her and her grandmother, his tall frame filling the hallway in a way which neither she, nor her grandmother, had ever done. He had a presence, and she'd forgotten about it. The appearance of Amber in the hallway, all large eyes and ethereal beauty, brought her back to the present.

"Rob! What are you doing here?" asked Amber.

Rob shook his head. "Not you, too." He sighed. "I'm here because David asked me to come."

"David?"

"Yes, David. Your husband."

Amber looked like she'd recovered. "I know who David is! What's happened? Is everything all right?"

"He's fine. He's still in Shelter Springs." His usual kind voice replaced the cool tone he'd used with Flo. He'd always been close to his youngest sister, and he obviously wanted to reassure her. "He says to tell you that Aimee sends her love."

"Aw, I miss my darling niece. Like you must miss your—"

"But he asked if I'd pick you up," interrupted Rob quickly.

Flo frowned. Rob might be a cheating bastard to her, but he was the kindest brother, and she'd never heard him interrupt Amber before. Not even when Amber was at her wackiest.

"What were you going to say, Amber?" asked Flo. "Rob might miss what?" Or who, she thought to herself.

Amber blushed and looked nervously at Rob. She shook her head.

"David reckoned you'd have walked to Flo's," continued Rob, as if Flo hadn't spoken. "And the storm is only going to worsen."

Amber smiled at the thought of her doting husband. "How come my husband knows so much about me?"

"I don't know," said Rob with a smile. "It's almost as if he loves you or something."

Amber beamed. "Yes, he does."

Flo's heart tweaked a little, and she looked away. So much love and none of it for her. "Well, you'd best get going then." She gave Amber a quick hug. "Thanks for coming and getting me started."

"I'll be back when I can. And Maddy and Gabe will, too. We'll all pitch in and help." Amber turned to her brother. "Won't we, Rob?"

Rob raised his eyebrow in question at Flo. "That's up to Flo."

Amber turned to Flo. "You *will* accept Rob's help, won't you?"

Flo shot Amber a dark look. Amber knew full well that Rob was the last person she'd accept help from. They both knew. "No. But thank you all the same," she added. She might hate the man who'd broken her heart so many years before, but she could be polite and grown up about it.

"Why not?" asked Amber.

Flo lost control of the tumult of emotions which surged through her whenever Rob was around. "Because I don't want him around." Her heart pounded, and she regretted the words as soon as they'd escaped, like steam, relieving the pressure but scalding everyone in sight.

Rob sucked in a sharp breath. "Right, I guess that's our cue to leave. Amber? You ready?"

Amber was looking worriedly from Flo to Rob and then back to Flo again.

Rob disappeared outside onto the porch.

Amber ignored Rob's question and gave Flo a hug and held on tight. "I'm sorry," she whispered.

"It's okay. I shouldn't have said that, but I feel you guys are pressuring me to do something I don't want. Amber, after what happened, I don't want anything from your brother."

"I just want the people I love to love each other."

"That only happens in fairy tales."

"No, no, it doesn't. I won't believe it. I won't *let* it be like that."

"Please, Amber, just leave me be. I know what I'm doing." And right there was the biggest lie of all.

While Amber went to collect her things, Flo was drawn to the porch, her eyes fixed on the dark shape of Rob's back. She knew her words had hurt him. And she felt guilty, despite the pain which she still nurtured and kept close—because how else could she protect herself?

"I'm sorry, Rob. That came out harsher than I meant it to."

His shoulders relaxed a little, and he turned slightly and looked over his shoulder at her. The dim yellow light of the outside light caught his face. It made his gaze warmer somehow. She swallowed.

"It's okay. I only hope that one day you'll forgive me."

Amber's arrival on the porch, carrying too many bags, saved Flo from answering. Amber juggled the bags as she tried to pull on her raincoat. Flo avoided Rob's eyes, but could feel his gaze on her as if it were a physical thing. It had always been like that. Some things, it seemed, never changed.

Amber yelped as a drip turned into a river of water as it broke through the rust in the porch roof. Was it Flo's imagination or was there more rain gushing through the holes in the porch? Amber put up her umbrella and grinned at Flo. "I'll be around again as soon as I can. But we've made a start." She gripped Flo's arm. "And don't forget to look for the key for the—"

A tearing sound from above interrupted Amber. Rob and Amber looked up. With one quick movement, Rob pushed Amber back into the hall, where she stumbled into Flo's arms as the porch roof came crashing down, along with a waterfall of rain.

Without a thought, Flo rushed out into the pouring rain and grabbed Rob's arm as he threw aside a rusting piece of corrugated iron, which had narrowly missed his head. He pointed to it, his eyes ablaze.

"Are you okay?" shouted Flo above the sound of the thundering rain. She could hardly see him in the gloom, as the porch light had gone the same way as the roof. All she could see were angry eyes and rain-slicked hair and body.

"Amber could have been killed, Flo! Amber or you! This has got to stop right now!"

She released her grip on his arm and stepped away. "I guess you *are* okay."

"Come in, you two!" shouted Amber from the hall. "You're both going to get soaked."

"Too late for that," said Flo, relieved to release Rob's angry gaze and step back into the house. She busied herself taking off her over-shirt and tossing it into the tray meant for umbrellas. She kept her gaze averted for a moment as she tried to slow her pounding heart. Rob was right, but she'd be damned if she'd admit it. Suddenly, she felt the tight grip of Rob's hand on her shoulder.

"Don't turn away from me again, Flo. This time it's serious. This place is a death trap, and it's about time you did something about it."

She lifted her chin angrily. "Don't you think I'm trying?" She took his hand and pulled it from her shoulder. "Don't you think I work every moment of every day to earn money to keep me, my house, my garden afloat?"

"It's sinking now," murmured Amber after peering out at the soggy lawn. She shot Flo an apologetic look. But Flo's gaze was firmly on Rob, who held up his hand to pacify her.

"Don't you hold up your hand to me, Robert Connelly, as if I'm some kind of mad dog that needs calming down!"

"He's only trying to help, Flo," said Amber, looking anxiously from one to the other. Flo sighed, exasperated. She knew Amber hated scenes, especially scenes between people she loved. Which meant virtually everyone in Amber's world.

"I know, but I don't need help." She turned away because she didn't want either of them to see she was lying or to see that her eyes were filled with tears. She waited for one of them to contradict the lie. But neither said anything. It was up to her. She looked up to the ornate plaster ceiling and blinked, willing the tears to disappear. She'd read somewhere that you couldn't cry if you looked up. She turned to them slowly and gave them a weak, rueful smile.

"Perhaps it would be more accurate to say I don't *want* help."

"No one wants help, Flo," said Rob, in a deep soothing voice which made a small place, deep inside of her, melt a little. "But sometimes you have to take it. You give to people all the time. It's about time you accepted something from them."

Damn. She couldn't stop her lips from trembling. She didn't trust herself to speak. All she could do was nod, as she thought about all the work which needed doing on the house.

She sniffed and cleared her throat. "Well, I guess the porch…" She trailed off as her voice threatened to break.

"The porch, yes," said Amber, gamely poking her head out the open door. "That would be an excellent start. Very good indeed. Yes." She nodded, over-keen to get this scene over and move things onto a pleasanter footing.

Flo couldn't help smiling, understanding exactly what Amber was doing, and caught Rob's answering smile. "It would be a good start," she said to Rob.

For a moment, that little place inside of her which had melted at his voice, melted a little more under the tender gaze of his eyes. Then Amber moved, and the spell was broken.

"Brilliant!" said Amber.

Rob looked from Amber to Flo once more. "I'll be back in the morning to assess the damage. We'll have it fixed in no time."

"But I can't—"

"I don't want money. Actually, you'll be doing me a favor. I have skilled men waiting to begin work on a project in

Christchurch. They can work here until the next project is ready."

He stepped away and turned to look outside. "Let's get going, Amber. I'll see you tomorrow, Flo. Bright and early."

"Right," Flo said. "And thank you!" she called out to Rob and Amber's receding backs as they ran across the soggy lawn toward the front gate where Rob's four-wheel drive was waiting. Rob waved a hand in acknowledgement before opening the gate for Amber.

Flo watched them leave. Then she glanced across at where she'd seen the stranger earlier and briefly wondered whether he'd been looking at her, the house or whether it had been a random moment. Random, she decided, as she looked up to the open sky where once the porch roof had been. The entire structure had twisted off its steel supports.

Rob had been right. It could have been very serious if he hadn't had pushed Amber out of the way. She shuddered at the thought of Amber being hurt. She would never have forgiven herself. And if Rob had been standing slightly to the left... She closed her eyes with a gasp as she felt the pain which he would have felt. It sliced inside her, and in that moment she knew she'd never be free of Rob Connelly. Whether she liked it or not, and she didn't, he occupied a place in her heart which would be forever his.

But that didn't mean she'd risk the pain of rejection again. Guilt motivated Rob—that much was clear. If he'd left her once for another woman, he could do it again. And that would kill her.

Bright and early, she thought, as she gave one last sweeping glance around the garden, which was being hammered by the rain. In the meantime, she thought, as she closed the door on the wet night, she had work to do. She had guests to feed, rooms to clean, baking for the café to do. And then, tomorrow, there was the decorating, the accounts,

21

potting the plants she sold at the weekend market and a repeat of today's chores—the list was endless. She felt as if she were treading water with one arm tied behind her back and she was slowly—inch by inch—slipping under.

Bright and early. She repeated Rob's words. Despite her initial determination to keep Rob Connelly out of her life, she felt relieved. Maybe, just maybe, he'd thrown her a lifeline.

2

Rob Connelly stood at his father's library window and surveyed the scene outside. Belendroit had been a place of peace and beauty for as long as he could remember—especially in the spring. From the gardens, a rambling confusion of colorful flowers and shrubs, to the spreading trees beyond, dangling the lanterns which had given their bay its name, Belendroit lived up to the meaning of its French name—beautiful place. But now the place was a hive of activity. Archaeologists, headed by Maddy, his brother Gabe's wife, walked around the gardens, loudly discussing how to deal with the damage the storm had wrought on the dig currently underway close to the property's boundary. The infectious sound of his niece's laughter floated up from the beach and he could hear his father arguing forcibly on the phone above the blaring of a trumpet from his favorite jazz track.

Rob slid the sash window closed—at least he now only had his father and the radio to contend with—and turned to face David, Amber's husband, who sat on the other side of the desk.

"Sorry about that, David. I guess I'd better get myself set up with office space in Christchurch sooner rather than later."

"No problem," said David. "I'm not sure I'll ever get used to the amount of noise the Connellys make when they're all together." He frowned. "Or even when they're on their own."

Rob grinned. "We're a noisy lot. I'm the quiet one in the family, and it's definitely taking me time to get used to the Connelly chaos at Belendroit again."

David narrowed his gaze, and Rob braced himself. He knew from past experience that when David focused on something or someone, he rarely held back. "I'm surprised you came home. We all are."

The 'we' had Rob puzzling, not for the first time, at how David and Amber had ended up together. They were like chalk and cheese. He'd known David at university and had always got on well with him but never, in a million years, had he imagined him with Amber. But, it seemed the old adage of opposites attract was true in this case, and he'd never seen his little sister happier.

"I have my reasons," said Rob carefully.

"Yes, Amber's told me them."

Rob frowned. It seemed his little sister still couldn't keep family secrets. Although, he guessed, David was one of the family now. "It's time to put down roots and there's only one place I can imagine doing that."

"Belendroit." David glanced out the window to the trees from which lanterns hung, welcoming all-comers. "It certainly has a powerful pull for your family. Like Rachel, you've returned after a long time away. Some, like Amber and Gabe, have never left. And those of you who have left— Max and Lizzi—return as often as possible. That only leaves Cameron, who I've never met."

"No, Cam didn't go to uni. He left here as soon as possible. My mother called him a free spirit. My father wasn't so kind. I'm hoping he'll come home for the anniversary of Mum's passing. It coincides with the Festival of Lights and would just be…" He shrugged. He wasn't used to opening up to family and friends, especially about emotions—he liked to keep those to himself. "I don't know."

David nodded briskly, obviously not wanting to hear any emotional confession from Rob, either. "I hope he comes for Amber's sake. It would mean a lot to her."

"It would mean a lot to us all, because he's the last one. Jonny never made it home. Anyway, let's get down to business." Rob tapped the building plans. "I definitely want to be a part of this. If you need a partner, that is."

"I don't *need* a partner, Rob. But I'd like to work with you. Amber's taught me a lot about family and you are the brother I never had. So, let's do this."

Suddenly the door burst open and Jim Connelly stood there, his thick white hair messy where he'd been pushing his fingers through, waving an iPad at the two men as if it were the devil. "This thing doesn't work properly!"

Rob took it from his father. "What do you want to do?"

"Amber set up Facebook for me. She reckoned it would be a way of connecting to my old mates. But I can't make it work."

"Because you're in the wrong place." A few taps and swipes soon had the correct screen displaying. Rob handed it back to him and showed him how to use it. "See? There's that woman who used to be in the amateur dramatic plays with you. She wants to be your friend."

Jim's face lit up. "Does she indeed?" And he returned to the kitchen with a broad smile on his face.

"Anyway, as I was saying," said Rob. "This project is exactly the kind I'm looking for. I may have made my money through finance, but my first love is property."

David stood up and held out his hand. Rob grinned and shook it. He loved David's formality. "Here's to a profitable future," said David. "A profitable future *with* family," he added. Even if Rob hadn't noticed the differences in David before, simply in that statement he could see the changes which marrying Amber had made to the man. He was no longer solely driven by profit.

"Yeah, you might run, but you can never get away from family," said Rob with a grin.

"True, and who'd want to? Amber and I want as many children as possible."

Rob laughed. "Good on you. I've always wanted a big family, too. At one time I thought... well..." He tailed off, realizing he was about to reveal those conversations he'd had with Flo about how they'd have at least nine children—one more than his father. She'd been all for it. But life had a habit of not turning out how he expected.

But it seemed David's logical mind had followed Rob's train of thought. David rolled up the plans, looked Rob directly in the eye, and tapped the plans on the desk as if coming to a decision. "So, what's happening with Flo?"

Rob raised an eyebrow. Another David direct question, but he hadn't seen that one coming. Then it clicked.

"No doubt Amber told you to ask me."

"Yep," said David, not even bothering to deny it. "And I can't go home without an answer. She told me how sharp Flo was with you the other night, which doesn't sound like Flo at all."

"Flo is kind and generous and loving... to everyone except me."

David grimaced. "Ah, a woman scorned and all that."

"Exactly. I made a hell of a mistake years ago and I have to live with that for every minute of every day. Flo won't let me forget it, and she certainly doesn't look as if she's going to forgive me."

"So, why are you still trying?"

"Because I have to. She might not forgive me, but I have to help her. It comes down to one word. Guilt."

"Amber thinks the porch collapsing was a sign from… well, I'm not sure from where, but she reckons it's a sign that things will change between you and Flo."

Rob shook his head. "My little sister sees signs everywhere."

David raised his eyebrows. "Tell me about it! But, I guess if the porch hadn't collapsed, Flo wouldn't have accepted your help. So at least you've got an opportunity to help her."

"True. I'm off there now to make a start."

"By yourself?"

"To begin with. I want to check it out first. And, at the same time, figure out what else needs doing in the house without Flo noticing."

"You've got your work cut out. I think Flo notices everything."

"I've always liked a challenge."

"I'll see your father before I leave."

Rob didn't follow David into the kitchen immediately. He felt uncomfortable after talking about Flo to David. In London he'd kept to himself and he'd forgotten what it was like to be surrounded by family. Strange that he should feel so connected at Belendroit, which was so isolated compared to London. Belendroit was surrounded on one side by the sea, and by trees on the other. The small community of Akaroa was a short distance away and New Zealand itself was thousands of miles from any other country. And yet here, he felt as if he were being jostled by family and feeling and companionship in a way he hadn't been in London—one of the biggest cities in the world. He grunted and turned away.

Flo. She was at the center of it all. Nearly ten years ago his mother had died, and he'd turned to Flo for love and support which, for whatever reason, had been denied him, and he'd gone looking elsewhere and found it. And that had been the biggest mistake of his life. He could still remember how Flo's beautiful green eyes had flooded with hurt. He'd felt as if he'd seen directly into her heart where all her hopes and dreams had been destroyed—by him. Hopes he hadn't even realized she'd had until that point. It had taken that one stupid act to reveal what she'd refused to admit to, and then it had been too late. And he'd had to live with the consequences of that one act, do the honorable thing, because he couldn't have done anything else.

Wanting to rid his mind of Flo's green eyes, which continued to haunt him, Rob walked through to the kitchen where Jim was showing David the people he'd found on Facebook. With no patience or interest in social media, David had soon left the house and Rob watched him roar off in his car down the road to Akaroa, where he lived with Amber.

Rob felt a pang of jealousy. He was surrounded by people who'd found their soulmates, had settled down and were living extremely happy lives. That left only him and Jim. He heard a crash and turned to see Jim had tossed his iPad onto the table. Luckily, a pile of newspapers broke its fall, and the screen didn't shatter. Rob sighed. Obviously, Jim was having difficulties with technology—again. He had a horrible vision of the two of them being grumpy old men together, alone in Belendroit. And then he remembered. There wouldn't be only the two of them shortly. They'd soon have company.

"Rob! That"—his father let out a stream of expletives

which a sailor would have blushed at—"iPad has gone wrong again."

"Got to go, Dad!" called Rob, picking up his phone and jacket. "See you later!"

~

"Rob," greeted Flo shortly at the front door, trying to stifle her visceral response to his presence.

"Flo," he responded, setting down a big box of tools on the grass. He peered up at the remnants of the porch roof, squinting into the sunshine which now bathed the area. The butter-wouldn't-melt-in-its-mouth weather, pretending that it would never have turned on a deluge like the previous night. Although the creek which flowed swiftly down from the high hills surrounding Akaroa was evidence to the contrary.

Flo looked around for his men, but there weren't any. "I thought you were bringing a team with you."

He caught her gaze, clamping it like a trap. She couldn't have looked away, even if she'd wanted to. And she didn't.

"I'm checking it out first. Besides, I didn't think you'd appreciate a team of builders descending on you."

"You're right. Just you descending on me will be more than enough." She'd meant the words innocently, but winced at their double entendre and the twinkle in his eye.

She blushed and looked away, unable to hold his gaze.

"Well, I won't keep you talking," she said. "No doubt you'd like to get on. Shout out when you'd like a cuppa and a slice of cake."

His grin hadn't faded. "Sure will."

She grunted and left him to it, going upstairs to strip the beds of the visitors who'd left that morning, in readiness for tonight's bookings. At least she had a steady stream of visitors since Maddy's intervention with the accounts and publicity. But it still wasn't enough to maintain an old house like this. In an effort to increase her income she grew herbs which were sold at the farmer's markets, baked cakes and muffins for Amber's café and ran evening classes in home economics. She felt like a hamster in a wheel—forever busy but going nowhere.

She turned on the vacuum cleaner and set to work, relieved to have physical work to channel the emotional turmoil that just knowing Rob was in her house had created. But there didn't appear to be enough vacuuming, lugging of bed linen, polishing or dusting in the world to banish the thought of him from her mind. She looked out the window, trying to persuade herself that he dominated her thoughts because of the banging and crashing sounds coming from the front door as he made short work of the remnants of the porch roof. But the sight of his shirt pulled tight over his shoulders as he man-handled a large piece of corrugated iron, bypassed her mind and went straight to her gut, causing a flip of desire which couldn't be misconstrued. She stepped away from the window. She had to pull herself together.

By the time she'd returned downstairs to take a batch of cakes out of the oven, she found Rob had come inside and had made himself a cup of coffee. He poured one for her. "Hope you don't mind me making myself at home." He held out a cup to her. She took it and sat down. "I've finished the demolition bit and am ready to build it up again. Trouble is…" He pulled a face.

Her heart sank as she took a sip of her coffee. "What?"

"It's exposed weakness in the spouting. It all needs replac-ing. And some of the weatherboards are rotten where the rain's got in through the rusting roof."

It seemed easier to take another sip of coffee than to speak.

"To be honest, Flo, I'm surprised that the council hasn't come down hard on you. Surely they've done inspections for your license?"

She was silent for a few moments, taking sugar she didn't want and stirring it into her coffee. "They have." She raised her eyes and caught his alarmed ones. "I've got until the end of the year to put things right."

"And you're going to?"

"That depends."

"On what?"

"On whether I can keep the committee coming here. I've earmarked their payments for the new electrics."

His brow furrowed. "You need new electrics, too?"

She sighed and rose, swilling out the remnants of her coffee down the sink. "Let's face it, Rob, I pretty much need to replace everything around here. A new me wouldn't go amiss either."

She jumped as he squeezed her shoulder gently. She stared at the sink, not daring to turn around, closing her eyes against the onslaught of warmth and emotion his touch ignited. How could such a simple thing as a man's touch create such feelings? But it wasn't just any man's touch—it was Rob's. And that had always had this effect on her.

"All you have to do is ask, Flo, you know that." His voice was gentle, the kind of voice which curled its way around obstacles without you even realizing, melting them. She blinked and turned around. He was much taller than her and looked down at her with narrowed eyes, as if expecting her to explode, or shake off his hand, which still rested on her shoulder. She did neither.

Instead, she placed her hand on his. His eyes widened in surprise. She tilted her head so her cheek rested on top of both their hands and closed her eyes. She wished she could stay like that forever, because in that moment the years

31

rolled away, obliterating all the pain and heartache she'd suffered, and there were just two people who mattered—him and her, in love. And then he broke the spell by making a sound somewhere between a groan and a gasp as he stepped closer to her. His breath warmed her cheek.

"No," she groaned and tore herself away. This was madness. She couldn't allow herself to be fooled by kindness. Rob was a kind and generous man. That was all. And that would never be enough for her.

She turned away from him, flicked on the taps, and began to fill the sink to wash the cups.

"Leave that." He turned off the taps, and she clutched the sides of the sink with wet hands.

"Why?"

"Because we need to talk."

"We have nothing to talk about. Everything that needs to be said *has* been said."

"No, it hasn't. *You* might have had your say, but you've never listened properly to me."

"But—"

"No buts. What I did was unforgivable. And I don't expect anything from you except maybe understanding."

"You left me for another woman. Someone prettier, someone with charm and sex appeal. I get it. It's not exactly rocket science."

"I left you because I was dying inside. My mother had just passed away, and I needed something which you weren't prepared to give."

Flo's lips felt dry as she opened them. "What?"

"Yourself. Even as a kid you were self-sufficient, never risking giving yourself to anyone in case they could somehow get to you and rob you of something important. I never understood it, and I still don't. But that day, when I came to you after Mum's funeral, I needed more than you were prepared to give."

She closed her eyes at the memory of how Rob had appeared on her doorstep that afternoon, distraught and needing her in a way she couldn't face. "We made love. I thought that would be enough."

"I needed more."

"I'd never seen you like that. It was scary."

"You'd never seen me needing emotional support before. I wanted love, and you refused to even say the word."

"But…" Flo trailed off as she tried to recall the events of that afternoon, which she'd spent what felt like a lifetime suppressing.

"I told you I loved you, and what did you say?"

She shrugged. "I can't remember." Although she did, but she didn't want to remember.

"Then let me refresh you memory. You joked. You told me you loved your dog, and that was it."

"I didn't mean it how it sounded. I was never any good at expressing myself."

"I reckon you expressed yourself pretty loud and clear then."

"No, Rob, I'm sorry. I meant that love for me is something hard."

"Love isn't hard."

"It is for me. I was raised by my grandmother, who cared for me and nurtured me, but she was never demonstrative, or ever told me she loved me. And she was all I had."

"Because your parents left."

There was that flick, like an elastic band against skin, in her heart. "Yes, my parents left. I guess I…" She couldn't continue. She never talked about her parents, and she certainly never talked about love.

"I guess you're scared to love in case someone leaves you.

Like your grandad. Like your parents. Like I did." He reached out and caressed her cheek. "But I'm here now, Flo, and I'm not going anywhere."

"Why?" The word emerged like a wail. "Why are you doing this?"

"Because I owe you, and because I still care about you. Can't we begin a new chapter in our lives? Me, helping you out with the house, and us becoming friends again."

"I don't know how I'm going to do that."

"One step at a time." He paused. "How about you let me help you out and I'll come here, bring my team and we'll get your house sorted out. No conditions, no demands. We just hang out together, talk, reminisce and, most of all, look to the future. Agreed?"

She nodded, and pressed her lips together, unsure she could speak as a wellspring of emotion threatened to erupt.

"Good." He stepped away, as if sensing her disquiet. "Then I'll get on."

THERE WAS something solid and reassuring about Rob, Flo thought as she continued to work in the kitchen. It wasn't simply hearing him talk on the phone to his men or builders' supply companies as the afternoon progressed, or the sound of hammering and sawing as he went about repairing the porch—it was simply his presence. It took her back to the time when they were kids. She'd always felt like she could cope with anything if he was around. In the end, she'd discovered she could cope with anything without *anyone* around—by herself. Because she couldn't trust anyone else to stick around. Even so, she couldn't deny it felt good to have him back in her life. It made her feel not quite so alone. Even if she was.

By six o'clock, the sun had passed below the clouds,

which had softened the afternoon light, and cast a rich, golden light over the harbor and town. Flo had ticked off the many jobs on her list, including preparing for the monthly folk evening which she hosted. She grabbed a couple of beers, and went to find Rob. He was packing up his things.

"Is it okay if I leave these behind?"

"Of course. You're doing me a huge favor, so you can leave whatever you need in the shed if there's room. Or there's the old garage you could use, too. How did you get on?"

"Good. It won't take long to get the porch fixed. But the rest?" He shook his head.

She really didn't want to talk about the shortcomings of her home right at that moment. She wanted to keep that warm feeling his presence gave her for just a bit longer. She held up the beers.

"Fancy a beer?"

He grinned and nodded, as if he knew exactly what she was doing. He twisted off the cap and took a long drink. She joined him and suddenly remembered the last time they'd shared a beer together. It had been the summer when she was nineteen. She shivered. It could have been the cold lager, or cooling breeze, but most likely it was the way he was looking at her, just as he had when she was nineteen.

"Cold?" asked Rob, that sexy look still lingering in his eyes.

"Not really." She shrugged. "Feeling kind of good, actually."

He smiled. "That makes two of us. Nothing like a bit of honest labor."

She smiled and turned away. "Let's go around the back. People will be arriving soon for the folk club."

They walked in companionable silence through the house to the back deck on which Flo had arranged extra chairs. When the double doors were opened, the deck served as extra living space. She sat in a chair and he stood opposite her. She suddenly felt shy and took another sip of beer.

"Are you staying for folk club?" she asked.

"Do you want me to?"

"I wouldn't have asked if I didn't."

He nodded, satisfied. "Then yes, I will." He took another swig of his beer, the other hand firmly pushed into his jeans' pocket.

They could hear people approaching, taking a shortcut from the center of town along the beach. Someone strummed a guitar as they walked, yet another sang while others chatted, their laughter flowing towards them.

Rob huffed out a laugh and leaned against the deck's pillars. "This takes me back. Last time I stood here like this, waiting for people to arrive for the folk night, must have been when your grandma was alive."

"I guess you didn't listen to folk music in London. There would have been far hipper things going on."

Rob grinned. "Yep. So hip that no one called them hip."

"Oh, well, that's me, stuck in the dark ages."

He was silent for a moment, studying her. "No, you're not."

"Come on! My favorite things are gardening, cooking and looking after people. I enjoy the wrong things and say the wrong words."

He reached out and touched her hand. "No, they're not wrong. They're perfect."

The sun gave one last blast of crimson light, highlighting the features on his face and the hand which touched her. Energy—pure and hot—surged inside of her, kick-starting something she didn't want to think about.

Her friends' laughter drifted closer. She looked up, and

they waved. She waved back and turned to Rob. "Perfect for me, perhaps, but not for anyone else."

He grinned and withdrew his hand, but not before brushing it along her arm. "You're one of a kind, Flo. And that's exactly the way I'd like to keep it."

His words both shocked and touched Flo, but also confused her. What did he mean exactly? That she was an oddity, but one he liked? But there was a possessive note in his words. Before she could respond, the gate was flung open and her friends tumbled into the garden, calling out greetings and giving hugs. She'd find out later.

ROB HAD FORGOTTEN what it was like. He looked around the large room with the windows opening out onto the deck, which was also crowded with people. He knew most of them from school or work, or as friends of friends. It was like he'd never been away. It felt good.

He took a sip of his cold beer and placed it on the wooden floor beside him.

"Room for a little one?" He looked around to see Amber kneeling beside him.

"Always room for my little sister." He scooted along, and Amber curled up on a patchwork cushion beside him. "No husband?"

Amber grinned. "Can you imagine David here?" She leaned in to Rob. "He'd hate it."

Rob laughed. "You're right. I think he'd do just about anything for you, except spend an evening listening to folk music."

"A little bit of difference is good, isn't it? Keeps us on our toes. Anyway, I'm surprised to see *you* here. Things must be going better between you and Flo than the last time I saw you both."

He shifted his gaze to Flo, who was deep in conversation with a tanned, handsome man in a white shirt and jeans. An archaeologist, he knew, from an earlier conversation he'd made sure he had with him, after seeing him eyeing up Flo. His smile dropped a little as Flo burst out laughing at something the man said.

"Yeah, well, I thought so, but Flo sure has a lot of friends."

"She's very popular," said Amber innocently. "Everyone loves her. She'll do anything for anyone and looks after backpackers like she's their mother hen, making sure they're cared for even if they don't have any money." Amber sighed and shook her head. "David says it's no wonder Flo's house is falling down when she has no idea about money."

Rob frowned at the thought of David and Amber talking about Flo. Despite his absence, he felt proprietorial and protective, and didn't like the idea of David criticizing *his* Flo.

"She's managed so far. I'm sure she'll be fine."

"Are you? We're not so sure. We're pretty worried. I'm so glad you've come back."

"Me too, me too."

They stopped talking as someone struck up some notes on a guitar and then a mandolin began to play. Suddenly, Flo began to sing and Rob stopped thinking altogether. He'd always known she had a wonderful voice—whether talking or singing—but it had changed, developed somehow in the years he'd been away. The traditional song she sang was an emotional song of longing and she poured herself into it. He never cried, but he could feel the pinpricks behind his eyes as her soulful voice filled the room, finding every vulnerable nerve ending and tweaking it until there wasn't a dry eye in the house. On the last note, she opened her eyes, and she was facing him, her green eyes dark as they looked at him. He was spellbound.

For a moment her voice filled the air, hanging in the space between them, before fading away. Then people began to applaud and cheer. She looked away then and grinned at her friends as the moment passed.

But it hadn't passed for him. He felt as if she'd told him something deeply personal, conveyed her feelings to him, and he'd received the message loud and clear. He'd hurt her, and he wasn't sure she'd ever forgive him. The happiness he'd felt earlier in the evening faded and he slipped out the room as soon as he could. He went outside to the porch to have a last look at his handiwork before going home. Suddenly, he realized he wasn't alone. He turned to find Flo standing in the doorway.

"You're leaving," she said.

"I've an early start tomorrow."

"Weren't you going to say goodbye?" she said, glancing at the car keys he held in his hands.

"You seemed too busy."

"I wasn't busy. I was talking to friends."

"Well, whatever. I didn't want to interrupt."

She twisted her lips and he could see she was upset. "Sure."

"Thanks for a lovely night."

"You're welcome. I'm glad you stayed."

The sound of the others in the back of the house seemed to recede, and he knew he couldn't leave without saying what he'd intended to tell her all evening.

"I'm sorry, Flo."

Shock briefly registered across her features before she took command of her expression once more. "Sorry? For what? For not mixing with our friends?"

"No, I'm sorry for what I did to you. I'm sorry for"—he shook his head—"having an affair with Cate."

She grunted in surprise. "I guess my reply should be 'apology accepted'. But you know? I don't think I can."

"You don't have to. But I do have to apologize because I did wrong. I should never have done what I did."

She swallowed. "You said earlier that I wasn't there for you when you needed me. And it's true. I couldn't give you what you needed. But Cate could. She offered you everything."

"And I took it. She said she loved me, but I soon knew I'd made the biggest mistake of my life. But, by then, it was too late."

"She was pregnant." Flo swallowed and pasted on a bright smile. "And how are your wife and son?"

He narrowed his eyes. Did she really not know? "Cate died, Flo, didn't you know?"

He could see it in her eyes that she hadn't known. She shook her head and looked away. "No, I didn't know. I don't know why Amber..." she trailed off.

"Maybe because you didn't give her the chance?" Rob could just imagine Amber trying to broach the subject of Rob's wife and Flo closing the subject down. Amber certainly wouldn't have pushed it. She was far too gentle. "We split up long before she died. Our marriage was a mistake—a terrible mistake. And I'm so sorry for all the pain it caused you."

"Oh!" The sound caught in her throat, cut off as soon as it had been uttered. She shook her head, her thick wavy hair tumbling around her face and shoulders, her large eyes dark, like an injured animal. "I... I have to go," she said, and closed the door on him.

He stood there for a few moments to collect himself. Then he turned and walked across the garden to his car. It was only when he'd started the car that he realized he hadn't told her everything. But what did it matter, he thought wearily? She'd find out soon enough.

3

---

*R*ob looked out across the waters of Akaroa Harbour to Belendroit, its chimneys just visible above the trees which surrounded it. The small bay, named after the lanterns which his mother had insisted be hung from the trees, was lined with yellow sand, which looked like a smile from his vantage point.

"It's an amazing view, isn't it?" said Amber, leaning against the balcony railing of her house.

"Sure is. And so is your place." He turned his back on the view and looked at the house, which was part modern and part cottage—a hybrid house which David had designed and built to suit both his and Amber's tastes. "And there was me thinking nothing much changed around here. This house wasn't here when I left. David has combined the styles well. The photos you sent didn't do it justice."

"It's fantastic. I can see everything that's going on from here. I can still be part of the community and know what's going on, but we've got a bit of distance, which David likes."

"If you know everything, perhaps you'll tell me about Flo. How come she hasn't married and had kids by now? I always thought that she'd have a family as soon as she could. She always wanted children. Lots of them."

Amber's smile dropped, and she blinked, as if hiding something. She shrugged awkwardly. "When I say I know everything, I don't think anyone could really know Flo. She keeps things pretty close." She bit her lip as if indecisive. That wasn't like Amber.

"Come on, what is it?"

She shrugged. "All I know is that Flo's done a U-turn on children. She says she never wants any."

"Flo said that?"

"Yes, I know, it's weird. She used to say she wanted a big family, but that all changed, when I don't know. I just remember the subject came up a few months ago, and she said she never wanted children, and changed the subject."

Rob looked into the mid-distance as he tried to make sense of this news. He couldn't. "I guess she'll change her mind when she's in a relationship. Has she had any boyfriends?"

"Plenty of friends who are boys. But I'm not sure how much closer she got to any of them."

"What about that man who was hanging around her last night?"

"He's asked her out—I've heard him—but she always makes excuses. He'll give up soon. They always do."

A part of him was relieved. Not the generous part, that was for sure, but the possessive, macho part. "So there's no one on the scene at the moment?"

"No one has *ever* been on the scene. Well, not one person. She surrounds herself with people, as you know. She's always busy, but I kind of get the feeling she's lonely, too."

He most certainly didn't like the sound of that. Now for the difficult bit. He didn't like involving his little sister in his plans, but it was clear he needed help. He cleared his throat. "So, how do you think she'll feel if I tried courting her?"

"Courting?" Amber laughed. "Have you become Mr. Darcy all of a sudden?"

"Who?"

Amber shook her head. "Never mind." She patted Rob on the shoulder. "I reckon you should give your *courting* a go. See what happens. I don't hold out much hope, though. Flo seems pretty determined to lead an independent life."

"Since when?"

Amber shrugged. "Since as long as I can remember."

Sadness washed over him as he remembered the woman he'd once known, who'd wanted nothing more than to marry and have children. Yes, she'd always been independent, but they'd been inseparable from when they were young friends to their mid-teens when they'd started dating. Their relationship had grown in intensity until their last six months together, when it had become a physical relationship. And yet... she'd always held something of herself back, had put up barriers when he'd talked of love, as if she'd been afraid. And it had been that which had finally driven him away. Coming from a warm, demonstrative family who was big on love, he hadn't been able to understand her and had assumed she simply didn't feel for him, as he felt for her. But now he was older, maybe just a little wiser, and a lot more determined to understand the complex woman who was Flo.

"Well," he said, pushing himself off the railing. "I'd best get off."

"Good luck, Rob." Amber rolled onto tiptoes and kissed Rob's cheek. "I think you're going to need it."

~

FLO JUMPED when the bang on the door came, despite the fact she'd been expecting it all afternoon. She'd changed twice before putting on her first choice of outfit, something she always wore. She looked at herself in the mirror and grimaced. No matter what she did to herself, she always seemed to look the same. Shorter than average height but, unfortunately not petite with it. Her hour-glass figure was embarrassingly sexy, and she tried her best to hide it with loose tops and straight jeans—nothing tight that would outline her figure.

She pulled her thick, chestnut hair back in a ponytail for good measure and nodded at herself as if she'd done something satisfactory. There was another resounding knock, followed by the door opening.

"Flo? Are you there?"

She took a deep, calming breath. It was only Rob. A friend from the past. Nothing more. "Coming!" she called out, before kicking her discarded clothes out of the way and running out of her bedroom, along the corridor and down into the main part of the house. Most of her guests had left for the day. The few remaining were in the shared lounge at the rear of the house where they'd had their party the previous night. She could hear them chatting and laughing. She liked that.

At the turn of the stairs, she stopped and looked at Rob, who glanced up at that very moment. He could still take her breath away. Who was she trying to kid by thinking he was only a friend from the past?

"Rob," she said, running down the remaining steps and coming to a halt by the kitchen door. "Good to see you. Come on in."

But instead of following her, he nodded toward the front door. "You should keep it locked. Anyone could walk in without you knowing, like that bloke who was just walking by. I saw him glance at the house."

"Bloke? What bloke? Did he stop?"

"No."

"Well, then, he was probably just someone passing by. Nothing to get fussed about."

"My point is that you need to take care of yourself. I didn't like the way he stared at the place."

"My home is an open house for my guests. I can't keep it locked up like a fortress. That's not what this place is about."

His expression looked unusually firm. "You should have stricter rules in place. Just promise me that when you're on your own here, you'll keep the doors locked."

Flo inclined her head, but couldn't provide the requisite promise. "Don't worry about me." But maybe she would begin locking up when she was the only one here. She remembered the stranger she'd seen the other night, checking out her house.

"I can't help worrying about you. We have too much shared history, for me not to."

Was that all? Shared history? She opened the door to the kitchen, anxious to change the subject. "We can start in here." Rob shook his head in disbelief when she handed him a notebook and pen, and pulled out a laptop from his bag.

He looked around with a practiced eye. "This looks like the best maintained room in the house." He lightly kicked the skirting board with his foot and reached up and examined a piece of plaster.

"It's the engine room of the house. The extra money I earned from the archaeologists who board with me, after Maddy got the dig going at Belendroit, went into maintaining the kitchen. My home-cooking is a big drawing card," she said, unable to prevent a tone of pride from creeping in. She might fail on a whole range of things, but she was the best cook she knew. Apart from Rob's big sister, Rachel, maybe. But Rachel focused on haute cuisine—not Flo's thing at all.

"I can believe it. You always were an amazing cook. Just like your gran."

Flo was silent for a few moments. Trust Rob to notice.

"What's up?" he asked. "Did I say something wrong?"

"It just feels weird, you mentioning Gran. Apart from you Connellys, there's not many of my friends who knew her."

"This was my second home, remember? When I got sick of being picked on by my big brothers, and pinned down and being made up with blue eye shadow and nail polish by my big sisters, I'd take off here."

"You were always Gran's favorite."

"And she was mine."

Their gazes met, lost in the memories of a simpler time. Flo was the first to turn away. She cleared her throat. "Anyway, yes," she said, looking around the kitchen. "I've done the electrics in here, and have a new Aga, dishwasher, etc. All things I needed to get my license."

"Well, let's move on then, shall we?" said Rob. "Lead the way."

They moved from room to room, Rob balancing the laptop on the nearest surface to enter information about the rooms and what was required to bring them up to council standards. Flo was grateful that Rob was doing this with her. Anyone else and she'd have felt defensive about the state of the place. But he knew her, and he knew the house, and he was very thorough.

The last place they entered was the dining room. Flo had given up calling it the meeting room. She hadn't had time to finish stripping the wallpaper and the room looked worse than ever.

"What's this?" Rob asked as he came across the half-hidden safe behind the top layer of wallpaper.

"What it looks like. A safe."

"Strange place to have a safe, behind the wallpaper."

"Yes, I haven't figured it out yet. It must have been decorated after Grandad died. So Gran must have done it. But I can't figure out why."

Rob pushed the door and it rattled slightly. "What's in it?"

"I haven't been able to open it yet. I've got a couple of key rings full of keys and I'm working my way through them. But I've been busy."

"We've got time now."

Flo chewed her lip and glanced in the direction of the key rings which she'd brought into the room, but somehow had always been reluctant to try.

Rob followed her gaze, shot her a quizzical look, and picked up the iron ring upon which dangled what must have been at least fifty keys of varying sizes and ages. He flicked through them. "I had a summer job once at a locksmith. I reckon it would be one of these." He held the tips of three keys up to her. "Would you like me to try them?"

She didn't want him to. But she knew it wasn't rational because she had to find out eventually. But she had a horrible feeling she wouldn't like whatever it was she'd find hidden in the safe. People didn't hide anything good in a safe. No, she'd prefer to check it out by herself later. Then she could decide what she wanted to do about it.

"Thanks. But I'll check it out later."

Rob gave a grunt of grim laughter. "Why am I not surprised?"

"What do you mean?"

"Ever the independent person. Open it yourself. Keep any secrets to yourself."

"Well, and why not? They are *my* secrets."

He held up his hands in surrender. "Absolutely. And God forbid you share them with anyone."

"Rob! *I'll* decide what to do with my own stuff, just as you decide what to do with yours. This is *my* life you've stepped into. You might want to leave yours behind, but you can't expect to come into my life and take over everything."

If she'd expected a fight, she was disappointed. "Fair enough." He took a few steps and then stopped and turned to her. "But I haven't left everything of my life behind."

"Your furniture? I'd have thought Belendroit had enough."

"I don't intend to live at Belendroit forever. But, no, I don't mean furniture."

"Then what? You told me about your wife. And, despite what happened, I'm sorry that she lost her life so young."

"Yeah, well, it was a shock to everyone." He paused, and a feeling of dread welled up inside of her. Was he about to tell her he'd loved his ex-wife after all? That they may have been divorced, but that he still missed her? She didn't think she could bear it. "Flo, there's something I have to tell you."

She held up her hand to stop further discussion. "Look, I'm sorry I brought her up. That's your business, not mine."

He put his hand on hers. "Flo, please stop putting up barriers between us. I'm going to be around permanently now and I really want us to be good friends."

She swallowed. It was a weak description of what she felt, deep down. "Honestly?"

"No, I'm lying. I would like us to be *more* than good friends. When I came back here, one of the first things I wanted to put right was past wrongs. I messed things up with you big time and hurt you, and I'm truly sorry for that. I want to make up for it."

"And you are doing." She gestured to the house, desperate to change the subject from the personal.

"Flo." He reached out and grabbed her hand. She stilled

instantly. She should have retrieved it. She really should have. But somehow it remained in his large hand while his thumb swept over her sensitive palm. She shivered and sucked in a breath of air, which held the essence of him in it. She couldn't have averted her gaze from his eyes if she'd wanted to. "But it's not enough," he continued. "I'd forgotten, you see."

"What had you forgotten?"

"I'd forgotten how much I feel for you. I thought it was in the past, but seeing you, just being with you, has brought it all back again."

She licked her lips, willing herself to focus on the negative, *any* negative. "If it left so easily when you did, then maybe it will go away again."

He shook his head. "It never left, Flo. I just ignored it, and I'm not willing to ignore it any longer."

"I am, Rob. I have to." Despite the emotions which raged within her, the voice of reason won out and she withdrew her hand from his. "It has to be this way."

"Nothing has to be a certain way," he said.

She felt as if he were battering down her defenses with each gesture, each touch, each word. But what would that leave her with? Nothing. She'd be vulnerable, and she didn't think she could withstand any more rejections. "Yes, it does. It has to be this way because that's the only way I know."

"If there's one thing in my life I've learned, it's that nothing stays the same. Circumstances change and people change. We're free to make new choices, if we both want to."

She shook her head. Her voice of reason was having a raging argument with her instincts. She swallowed hard. "I can't, Rob. I need to be in control of my life. Without that, I don't know what…" She gulped as she realized she'd nearly told him what she'd told no one else. That without control she wouldn't be able to protect that vulnerable place within her, which she no longer allowed anyone near. She'd only done it once before, and the pain of rejection had nearly destroyed her. She couldn't take that risk again.

Rob frowned as he searched her eyes, as if understanding instinctively the thoughts which careened through her brain. "Did I do this to you? Was it me who made you so scared of what's in your heart?"

She clamped her hand against his, stopping him from caressing her. "Rob, please, for the love of God, just accept it. I don't know how much more I can take."

He nodded and withdrew. She released a tightly held breath. She was falling for him and there was nothing she could do except hold on tight to that sense of self-preservation which had always served her so well.

Just at that moment, an alarm on Rob's watch sounded, and he looked at it, as if shocked.

"What is it?" she asked. "You look as if you've seen a ghost."

He took a step away as if needing to distance himself from her, and his lips twisted into an expression of pained regret. "I almost forgot. Although how I could—" He didn't finish his sentence but simply shook his head again as if to clear it of confusion. "Anyway, I have to go."

"Go?" Had this all been a charade? Something he'd got swept away with and then this sudden withdrawal? "Go where? I don't understand. We haven't finished looking around the house."

"I know." He shuffled his feet as if, suddenly, he couldn't wait to leave. "We'll do it another time, but I have to go now."

She realized he hadn't answered her question, and she suddenly felt angry. After all that talk about wanting a friendship, his holding her hand, all the talk about how things can change, suddenly he'd had enough and was leaving.

"Sure," she said curtly, opening the door for him. "Don't let me hold you up."

"Flo," he said in a warning tone. "Whatever you imagine being the reason for me leaving, you're wrong. I don't regret any of the things I've said to you. In fact, there's a whole lot more I want to say."

She gave him a brief, tight smile. "Then I'll look forward to that another time."

He gave a dissatisfied grunt and twisted around, pushing his hand through his hair. She couldn't figure out how it could make him look even sexier. "I wouldn't leave things like they are between us unless it was urgent."

He was holding something back from her and she didn't have a clue what it was. "What could possibly be so urgent at four thirty on a Sunday afternoon?"

He sighed. "The flight from Auckland to Christchurch arrives at six."

"And you have to meet someone off it?"

"That's right."

"Your girlfriend, perhaps?"

He shot her a dark look. "Do you really think I'd be here, talking like I have been to you, if I had a girlfriend hidden away somewhere?"

"I don't know what to think. If you don't have a girl-friend, then why all the secrecy?"

A muscle twitched in his jaw as if he both wanted to speak, and didn't want to speak. He sucked in a deep breath, picked up his laptop, pocketed his phone and walked over to the door, which she was still holding open.

"Just remember this, Flo, I tried to tell you every day we've seen each other. And before that, I asked Amber to tell you, but she couldn't."

Suddenly, a feeling of fear crept into Flo's gut. "What is it? What's happened?"

"Nothing terrible. Actually, it's something very good. For me, at least. And I hope you will come to like it too. More than like."

"What? Tell me."

"I'm going to pick up my son from the airport. My son. Oliver. He's coming to live with me. A friend has brought him over."

"Your son. But… ah," she said, as suddenly all the pieces of the puzzle fell into place, forming a pattern she didn't want to see. "Your wife died."

He nodded. "Which means I can return to New Zealand. I've been living in England to be close to Olly, but now my wife is no longer around, we can come back to live in New Zealand."

Flo felt a chill envelope her, giving her an icy calm. She nodded, stepped away and picked up his car keys from the table and tossed them to him. He caught them with a quick sweep of the hand, his fist clenching around them, his expression questioning her, wanting to know more than she could tell him.

"Then you'd better get going," she said, again the false sense of calm filling her, for which she thanked God—even if it was temporary. She refused to let him see how much his news had got to her.

Their former intimacy had disappeared the instant he'd dropped the bombshell that he hadn't left his past behind him. And, more than that, he'd be bringing it with him. She could have kicked herself. She'd been so bowled over by Rob's presence that, if she had given his son more than the briefest thought, she'd somehow imagined his ex's family would look after him. But he was Rob's son. And he had a name. Oliver.

"Right." He gave a deep sigh and walked out the door. She closed it after him, too firmly. A photo fell off the hall table with a crash. Glad of the activity, she went and plucked a dustpan and brush from a cupboard and knelt down to clear up the mess. A sliver of glass sliced into her knee. She withdrew the shard and looked at the blood, feeling the pain only distantly. Because everything paled beside the pain that had sliced into her heart the moment Rob had mentioned his son.

His past had returned. It had never gone away. There would be no turning the clock back. Because he had a son who would be a permanent reminder of everything Flo had lost.

4

*I*t was midnight by the time Rob crept down the winding stairs from the attic room at Belendroit, where Olly had only just fallen asleep. Despite Olly's exhaustion, the time difference had kept him awake and hyped until it had taken the combined efforts of a talking book, flickering night light and what seemed like hours of hair stroking to encourage him to drop off.

As Rob made his way along the hall to the kitchen where his father, Amber and David were waiting, he couldn't help think that Olly's first meeting with the Connelly family had gone spectacularly badly. Olly had looked terrified when faced with the Connelly clan and Jim had over-compensated with warm embraces and loud laughter, which only had the effect of making Olly cry.

Even after Rob had told most of his family to go home, Amber still hadn't been able to comfort Olly. Strangely, it had been David's no-nonsense formality with which Olly had been most at ease. David hadn't tried to placate Olly or talk down to him and eventually Olly's little shoulders had stopped hitching up in convulsive sobs as he and David had looked through a book on New Zealand architecture together. On reflection, Rob wasn't sure whether it was David or the architecture which had soothed Olly most. Both were as unlikely as the other.

Amber jumped up as Rob quietly closed the kitchen door behind him. "How is he?"

"He's been asleep for half an hour. I waited that long because he kept falling asleep and then jumping awake as if he was scared of sleep." Rob rubbed his gritty, tired eyes.

Amber wrung her hands. "Poor boy, after everything he's gone through. I'm sorry I couldn't do more to put him at his ease."

"He'll be fine. He's a bit overwrought. Partly his mother's fault. She was terrified he'd become rough and so kept him inside most of the time and vetted his friends. Only quiet, studious ones could play with him. That's why I wanted to move back here. Give him a normal life."

Jim clapped Rob on the back. "Like the one we gave you. Good call, Robert. Good call. The little lad will be fine. Fresh air, good food and family around him. He'll be as good as gold in no time."

Rob raked his fingers through his hair with a sigh. "I hope so. I really hope so. If only Cate's parents hadn't changed my plans. I'd always intended to travel with him, but they couldn't wait to get shot of him." He shook his head.

"They shouldn't have done that," said Amber. "But at least you managed to find someone you knew to accompany him."

"Jim's right," said David. "He'll be fine. The Connelly family can be overwhelming. It might have been better not to have had Rachel, Zane, and their family and friends over. I think Gabe, Maddy, and the kids would have been enough. It was a lot for me to take in when I first got to know you all. Let alone a small kid from the other side of the world."

Rob nodded. "You're right. I should have thought it

through. I just wanted him to meet everyone. I wanted him to see the kind of life we'll live here, which we didn't have in England."

"It's understandable. But maybe give the kid some space over the next few days."

"You're right, David, and thanks. I appreciate your help. I think you made a better connection with Olly than any of us did. Including me."

"That's only because I didn't want anything from him, or expect anything. It'll be fine when everything settles down. You'll see." David turned to Amber. "We'd best be on our way."

"Night, Pop," said Amber, kissing Jim on the cheek. "And night, you," she said to Rob, giving him a hug.

"Thanks, Amber, thanks both of you. I appreciate your support."

"We love you, big brother."

"Speak for yourself," grinned David as he opened the front door for Amber.

Amber shot him a mock angry look. "I speak for both of us," she said, pausing on the front step, "when I say we love you and we love your little boy unconditionally and we'll do everything in our power to make you happy here, in your new life. You're not to worry. If you want anything, *anything* at all, just ring David."

"What?" asked David, as he followed Amber.

Amber ignored her husband's question. "We'll see you tomorrow, okay?"

"That would be great." Rob followed them outside. He glanced up at the small window in the eaves where a night-light shone, vying with the lanterns in the trees outside his window to brighten the darkness. "I've a feeling it'll be a long night."

"It'll all be all right, you'll see."

"I hope so."

"I *know* so," said Amber. "And I don't just mean Olly."

Rob did a double-take as he watched Amber and David walk to the car. He raised a hand in response to Amber's wave. He stood on the steps for a few minutes watching the taillights of David's car disappear around the winding road which hugged the harbor. Then silence fell, and he looked into the trees, still strung with the lanterns his mother had hung there so long ago. And he felt such a strange mixture of peace and nostalgia and, despite Olly's upset, for the first time in a long time he felt something else—hope.

His father's footsteps made him turn. "I'm glad you've come home, son. I've missed you."

"Missed you, too, Dad. I don't think I realized exactly how much until I came home."

Jim nodded. "That's the way it is, sometimes. Anyway, I'm off to bed now. Good night."

Rob lingered a few moments longer, glancing up to the attic room where Olly now lay, hopefully sleeping. And then turned back to the lights of Akaroa, automatically seeking the twin chimneys of Flo's house, darkly silhouetted against a star-sprinkled sky. Like Belendroit, it was one of the oldest houses in Akaroa and had all the grand old pretensions of size, including multiple chimneys. As a boy, he'd always turned to look at her house when he'd come outside. And, last thing at night, he'd always glance at it before returning inside. Flo was like a constant in his life. True north. He gauged everything else by her. There was no getting away from it, no denying it anymore. She was the only one for him. All he had to do was get past her defenses and make her see how right they were together.

He huffed a grim laugh. He had his work cut out on both counts. Maybe things would look brighter in the morning.

. . .

But, despite the bright sunshine of the next morning, things looked no better.

"What's he doing?" frowned Jim as he came and stood beside Rob, who was watching Olly, squatting on the beach, studying the sand, periodically poking his finger into it. Olly had refused to take off his shoes and wore his shiny leather school shoes, grey trousers with a crease down the middle and a shirt buttoned up to his neck. He looked the complete opposite of a kiwi kid.

Rob shook his head. "Looking at the sand, I think."

"Not much to see, I shouldn't have thought."

Rob tried to turn his father away from the sight of his son looking distinctly eccentric, but Jim wasn't so easily moved. "Is he well, Rob?" Jim's shaggy eyebrows dipped over his incisive gaze.

"Of course he's well. He's just not used to a big family, not used to the sea or the countryside."

"What *is* he used to?"

Rob huffed out a frustrated sigh. "Cities. Well, no, not even cities. I think he must have stayed inside a lot. Cate was always saying he had allergies, and refused to allow me to take him out on excursions to the zoo, or anything like that."

"Are you telling me, that boy"—Jim pointed at Olly who was now picking his way gingerly over to the grass, as if he'd never felt wet sand beneath his shoes before—"has spent his whole life cooped up in a townhouse in central London with only his mental mother for company?"

"Come on, Dad, she wasn't mental."

"Well, she wasn't sane either. There's nothing sane about incarcerating a young lad like that. It's positively Dickensian."

Rob couldn't contradict his father. When he'd arrived at Cate's townhouse at the agreed visiting times, Olly had always seemed a little reserved, but so at home in his own environment that no alarms bells had rung. Rob had quashed any qualms over the boy's supposed ill health. But now that he'd had a chance to talk to Olly's doctor, he'd discovered Olly was as fit as a fiddle.

"Well, he's here now and he'll adjust," said Jim. "No doubt it'll take a little time, be a little difficult for him, for us all. But he'll get there. I'm *sure* he'll get there. Kids are resilient creatures." Jim's frown deepened as he watched Olly. "Or at least you lot were."

Rob and Jim both gazed at Olly, who'd pulled a large white cotton handkerchief out of his pocket and was trying to wipe away the sand which stuck to his leather-soled shoes. Rob didn't need to be telepathic to know what Jim was thinking. There was nothing resilient about Olly.

"So," said Rob with false bravura, "I thought we'd stick around here this morning, get him used to the place, if that's all right with you?"

"Of course it's all right with me. I love having Belendroit full of family, you know I do. And I hope you stay here for as long as you like."

"We'll get our own place eventually, but for now it would be great because it's still school holidays, but I'm going to have to go back to work at some point."

"Ah, about that. You know I'll be more than happy to babysit, but I have got this op scheduled."

"When?"

"Next week."

"Next week? You didn't tell me that."

"You didn't ask. And I've a pre-op check tomorrow morning. But I wouldn't worry. I'm sure one of your sisters or brothers will help out. There's one thing we're definitely not short of, and it's family to babysit."

Rob was reassured. He'd done the right thing. Olly would find a home here, and be the kind of kid he was meant to be, the kind of kid he could never be in London. Fear tightened his gut, contradicting what his mind told him. Because he was afraid he'd done absolutely the worst thing for his little boy, uprooting him from everything he'd known. And it damn near broke his heart.

~

FLO FLUNG OPEN THE DOOR, expecting a delivery of paint. "Rob!" she exclaimed.

"Flo! Look, I'm sorry about how we left things yesterday."

"It was certainly a surprise. That your son was coming to live here in New Zealand. You might have—"

"Olly!" Rob called out, interrupting her. He turned behind him. "I'd like you to meet my friend."

Rob stepped to one side, revealing a slender, blonde-haired boy with the biggest brown eyes she'd ever seen. He reminded Flo of a baby deer. She remembered seeing the film Bambi as a kid and being devastated by its sadness. The feelings came flooding back as she gazed at this slight boy who bore little resemblance to his father and was dressed as if he were about to step into the hallowed halls of Eton. Everything Flo had been about to say—all her recriminations and blame—fled from her mind. Instead, she bobbed down to the boy's height, instinctively keeping her distance.

"Hello. I'm Flo. What's your name?"

He swallowed but held his head up high as if he refused to be beaten by his nerves. Her heart squeezed a little more.

"Oliver Connelly, miss."

She quickly suppressed a smile. He'd said his name quickly, as if responding to a roll call. And the 'Miss'? What on earth was that about?

Going with the formal vibe, she extended her hand. "Pleased to meet you, Oliver. I'm Miss Flo Pelletier, but I'd prefer it if you called me Flo. Everyone else does." She rose to her feet and glanced at Rob. "Even your dad calls me Flo, among other things, I'm sure." She shot Rob a wry smile. Her smile turned to a frown. Rob looked tired, as if he'd been up all night. She looked back at the boy. "Would you like something to eat? I do the best French toast in town."

"Yes, please." Oliver looked up at Rob for approval and Rob nodded and looked worriedly back at Flo. She could understand why. Rob had never been anything like as unsure or nervous as Oliver, and she wondered how he was coping.

"Excellent." She extended her hand for him to take and, for a moment, she wondered if she'd over-stepped the mark, put some kind of emotional pressure on the boy. But it was obviously the sort of gesture he was accustomed to and he immediately took it and they walked into the kitchen, followed by Rob.

She released the boy's hand and pointed to the stool at the kitchen bench. "Why don't you sit up there and I'll get us all something to eat."

She left Oliver to it while she went to the pantry to get some eggs. She glanced around to see him climbing gingerly onto the stool. His smart gray trousers draped in folds around obviously skinny legs, which dangled, unable to reach the footrest. He sat completely still, his hands clasped together in his lap as he looked across to his father. She supposed Rob was the one sure thing in the lad's fluid, ever-changing world, and she felt an overwhelming sense of sorrow and recognition. She'd been there once.

"Can I help, Flo?"

She gave Rob an appraising look and raised an eyebrow. "You can get yourself a coffee. You look like you need one."

Rob nodded. "Yeah, feeling a bit done in this morning." He pointed to the cupboard. "Is the stovetop espresso pot still in there?"

"Sure is." She smiled at Oliver, wanting to include him in

the conversation, and particularly wanting to make him feel secure. "Not much changes around here. So, how was your first night at Belendroit, Oliver?"

"He goes by the name Olly, don't you, son?" said Rob.

Olly nodded. "Fine, thank you."

Flo could hear the words, but knew he meant the opposite. Goodness, Rob was going to find his son challenging. Rob had always said exactly what he meant—what you saw was what you got.

"Which bedroom did you sleep in?"

Olly blinked. "Up at the top of the house."

"The attic room?"

Olly nodded.

"That was your dad's room." Flo turned to Rob. "You used to share it with Cam when you were boys, didn't you?"

Rob took the cue. He glanced around at Olly while he filled the coffeepot with water. "Your uncle Cam and I used to get up to some mischief there. We raced skinks, kept our pet wetas there, and once nearly burned the place down. We would have done if it hadn't been for my big sister Lizzi smelling smoke and turning the hose on it, and us." He grinned. "Our first science experiment literally went up in smoke."

Flo laughed. "I hadn't heard that story before."

"I'm not surprised. We managed to keep it from Mum and Dad. Dad still doesn't know that the house nearly burned down."

Flo whistled and noticed Olly's eyes were even larger than before.

"Yes, something definitely *not* to do. But about your pets? It's a wonder your skinks and weta co-existed. Do you know what they are, Olly?"

He shook his head.

"They are very cute—"

"My sister, Rachel, would not agree—" interrupted Rob with a grin.

"But strange," Flo conceded, "little animals." She nodded toward the garden. "We can go and see if we can find any later, if you'd like."

Olly looked out the window to where Flo had indicated, and his eyes widened. "You have a garden."

Flo and Rob exchanged looks. Flo wiped her hands on her apron and walked to the French windows, and opened them. A warm breeze flooded into the kitchen. "Yes, I have a garden. And I spend as much time in it as possible. Gardening is my favorite thing to do, closely followed by cooking."

She heard a thud behind her and she turned to see Olly had slid off the stool and had followed her up to the door and was looking outside. He looked up at her with such wonderment that she struggled not to laugh. "It's like a park."

"Why, thank you. I enjoy working on it, like to keep it producing for me and my guests, keep it smelling nice and looking pretty."

"Producing?"

"My veggie garden is a thing to behold."

"Can I see it?"

"Sure. How about we eat and then I'll show you around."

As Olly returned to his chair and Flo picked up the beater for the eggs, she did a double-take. Rob was looking from Flo to Olly and then back to Flo again. He shook his head as if he couldn't believe what he'd just seen and returned to the coffee maker, which was beginning to bubble. She'd find out later what he was thinking. But, in the meantime, these two needed food. And that was definitely one thing she could provide. And provide well.

By the time Flo slid three plates piled high with French toast and crispy bacon onto the table, together with a big jug of maple syrup, Olly had relaxed and was talking about the garden—or, to be precise, about the gardens he'd read about in books. Flo interjected from time to time, encouraging Olly, while Rob watched and listened. Rob looked better already, thought Flo.

She winced at the memory of her reaction when he'd told her about Olly. The wave of jealousy and insecurity had come out of nowhere, triggered by the knowledge that Rob's son—the reason he'd stayed with the woman with whom he'd two-timed Flo—had come to live in Akaroa. She glanced at Olly. But those negative feelings had instantly subsided when she'd first laid eyes on him. She always knew her maternal, caring side was strong, but hadn't realized quite how strong until she'd seen this little lost boy.

"How about your dad does the washing up while I show you the garden? We can look for wetas."

Flo stepped outside, not waiting for Olly's response. She imagined everyone was walking on eggshells around him and that he might respond more easily to someone acting normally. "Goodness." She stopped by the camellia hedge, running her hands over the fresh growth. "This needs a good prune."

"Yuck," said Olly, who she turned to find had followed her. "I hate prunes."

She managed to swallow a smile. "Not the kind of prune you eat. Come on, I'll show you what I mean." She opened the creaking door to the massive wooden shed in which she stored everything from secateurs to a water slide and looked around.

"Wow," said Olly, taking it all in.

Wow, indeed, thought Flo as she watched a slow smile spread over his face.

. . .

ROB TURNED off the hot tap just in time before the water spilled over the edge of the Belfast sink, distracted as he watched Flo and Olly. He was in equal parts relieved and concerned. How had Flo managed to ease Olly out of himself where he, his siblings, and his father had failed? They were part of a large family and Flo was an only child, and yet she'd instantly hit it off with his son.

He began washing up as Olly stepped out of the shed holding some pruning shears, followed by Flo. They fell into an easy step as they walked across the garden, with Olly's attention divided between looking up at Flo as she talked, and opening and closing the shears. Rob dropped the washing-up brush with a splash and gripped the sink again. What did Flo have that neither he nor his family possessed?

But he knew the answer. Her basic instinct was to nurture people, tend them as she would do her veggie garden —feeding them, giving them space within which they could grow. That she could also find it in her heart to nurture Olly, given who his mother was, was amazing to Rob. His heart swelled with feelings he'd spent far too long denying. There had only ever been one person for him—no matter how much he might try to sabotage their relationship.

He set to work cleaning up the kitchen with renewed energy. It was as if something had fallen into place, a puzzle whose pieces had been scattered but which now slid into place with an ease which astounded him. It had been there all along, but he'd been too blind to see it. He'd wanted to help Flo to appease his guilt for the hurt he'd caused her. But now he realized that his urge to help had a deeper root. He wanted her back in his life again. It was that simple, and that hard. But he knew enough about life to realize that he had no choice. If he, and his son, were ever to make a happy life for themselves, it had to include Flo. No question.

He wiped his hands on the towel as he watched Olly

kneel on the damp grass to smell the mint which Flo was bending toward him. There didn't seem to be any worry now about getting his smart trousers dirty. His face lit up. And so did Rob's as he filled the kettle.

"I THOUGHT you both might like a cuppa," said Rob, handing out the mugs of tea to Flo and Olly.

"I always like a cuppa," said Flo with a grin, taking a sip of her tea. "Um, you remembered. Nice and strong and no sugar."

"Of course I remembered. I've never forgotten anything about you."

"Dad," said Olly, frowning into his cup. "It's tea. I don't drink tea. Mummy said it's bad for me."

Rob took a deep breath, trying to contain his annoyance at his ex-wife's misplaced dietary beliefs. But he didn't want to contradict his ex to his son. "This isn't the bad kind of tea. This is mainly hot water with a dash of tea. I added a little sugar, as I know you're used to more sugary drinks."

Olly took a sip and blinked. Then he looked up with a smile. He held up the mug to Flo. "I'm drinking grown-up tea."

"I can see."

"Cool mug."

"I think one of my backpackers gave me it."

"Boss Lady," Olly read out.

Rob read the rest out. "Confident, Strong, Loving, Caring, Hero, Role Model, Leader, Helpful, Smart and Always Right. The Boss Lady!" He grinned at Flo. "That sounds about right."

Flo shrugged. "I've got to keep my guests in order somehow."

"And they obviously appreciate it."

Olly wandered off with his drink, following a butterfly. Flo and Rob turned to watch him.

"He doesn't drink tea?" asked Flo. "Definitely not a Connelly, then. You lot, like me, were brought up on it."

"Cate used to think fizzy drinks were okay. She really didn't have much of a handle on what was healthy, and what wasn't."

"And I suppose you do," said Flo.

He held her gaze. She was laughing. He wasn't.

"I'd go for natural anytime," he said. Flo turned away, a faint blush on her cheeks. "You're so good with him, Flo. My family—apart from David—was having a real hard time communicating with him. But you? I don't know how, but you instantly connected with him. I can't thank you enough."

"You don't have to thank me at all. I haven't done anything. You've got a great kid there. He's really interested in the garden and nature. He said he didn't go out much at home. They didn't have a garden. For real? You didn't have a garden?"

"No. We had separate apartments, which weren't too far from each other's. Cate didn't like me taking him into parks or zoos. Kept saying he was susceptible to things. He had a little asthma, but he seems fine to me, and the doctor confirmed it."

Flo grunted as she watched Olly.

"What was that grunt for?"

"Oh, nothing. Just thinking about Olly. It must be hard for him after so long being cooped up and over-protected." She turned from Olly to Rob. "You did the right thing, Rob, bringing him here."

"I know. I thought you'd understand. It makes it easier to ask you a favor."

She frowned. "What kind of favor?"

"The kind I wouldn't have asked if you hadn't said I did the right thing."

"Sorry, I don't understand."

"I thought looking after Olly until school started again would be easy with all my family around. Between them and my flexible hours, I thought it would be fine. But it turns out that Dad has a doctor's appointment tomorrow and has to go into hospital next week. Amber and David are on holiday and Rachel's in Wellington for the week. Maddy offered to look after Olly, but I know she's really busy. So…" He trailed off, suddenly aware that Flo's smile had dropped.

"You want me to look after Olly?" He didn't miss her incredulous tone.

"It's just that you said I did the right thing bringing him here, to you."

"I meant bringing him here, to New Zealand."

"Oh."

"Yes, 'oh'." Flo glared at Rob before walking across the kitchen. She turned to him, crossing her arms defensively. "That's really rich, Rob. You dump me, marry someone else, and have a child. Then you return here and expect me to look after said child. I can't even begin to imagine how you think that's reasonable!"

"When you put it like that, it doesn't sound so good."

"You can put it anyway you like, and it still won't sound good."

He stood up. "I'm sorry. I shouldn't have said anything. It's just…"

"Just what? Imagined I'm a soft touch?"

"No, it's not that, it's…"

"Believed that I can drop anything, at any time, to do something for someone? Hey? That what I'm doing with my life isn't worthy of respect?"

"No, Flo, it's not that either." He held up his hand. "Please, let me finish," he said gently, realizing the hurt which lay behind her anger. "What it is, is that you've done more for Olly in ten minutes than I've done in years. You've made him come out of himself while my family and I have been running around him, making everything so much worse. You've come in and enriched his life with one gentle word after another. You're incredible, Flo. Incredible. And that's why I wondered if he could hang out with you more."

Rob didn't think he'd ever seen Flo speechless before. She might have been quiet, far away in thought, or she might have been listening, her mind intent on what the speaker was saying, but here, right now, he could see that she was well and truly floored. She didn't know what to think and so she didn't know what to say.

"But, hey," he continued. "I'm sorry, I shouldn't have imposed on you because you are so amazing. That was wrong of me, especially given our history." He pushed himself away from the countertop, and walked over to Flo. She looked up at him, amazement making her green eyes golden. He couldn't help himself. He pushed back a strand of thick hair which had fallen over her face and pushed it behind her ear. "And that's a history I really wish had turned out differently. But I can't turn back the clock."

Her breasts rose and fell more swiftly against the tight, black t-shirt and he was so close he could see the pulse in her neck quicken. What he wouldn't give to pull her into his arms and to kiss her so thoroughly that there would never again be any need for words.

But he hesitated. She swallowed and spoke, breaking the spell. "No, not unless you take it apart. I guess you could do anything to a clock then."

"Maybe even mend it?"

He grinned, and she followed suit.

"Dad!" came a shout from the door. They both turned to

see Olly, saturated from head to foot, and a big grin plastered across his face—the first he'd seen on his son for many months. "I've found the garden hose!"

"Brilliant!" said Rob, and in two paces he was beside his son, grabbing hold of the hose from which water was pouring and turning it on Olly, who ran away screaming with laughter across the lawn. Of course, Rob let Olly grab hold of it and, eventually, he, too, was soaking wet. It seemed Olly's earlier reluctance to get dirty had been a reaction to his first close encounter with a beach.

Flo tossed Rob a towel, and she took another one over to Olly and first wiped his face and then his hair and put it around him. "I reckon you two need to go home and change."

"But then can we come back, Dad?" Olly looked at Rob. "Please? It's so much fun here."

Rob reached over and dried a smudge of dirt off Olly's face. "We can come back if Flo invites us some time, but Grandad will be waiting."

Olly's face dropped. "Oh."

Flo beckoned Olly over to him and leaned down. "Would you do me a favor, Olly?"

He nodded eagerly.

"Would you be able to come back tomorrow and help me with the gardening? I could do with another pair of hands to tidy things up."

"Yes, please. I'd like that."

"Are you sure?" asked Rob to Flo.

"Sure, I'm sure." Flo didn't take her smile off Olly's face. "I'd be glad of the company. Any time you can spare Olly, he's welcome to come over. If that's okay with you, Olly?"

He smiled and nodded and reached out for her hand. Rob's heart clenched because of all the might-have-beens, all the history they might have had together, but which he had ruined with his stupidity. But at least he had Olly, and he could never entirely regret what happened because his son was the result.

"Rob? Okay with you?" Flo turned her eyes, cool green again now, to him.

"Absolutely."

"When, Dad?"

"I have a meeting first thing tomorrow morning. I'll drop you at Flo's then, if Flo's sure."

"Sure, I'm sure."

"Tomorrow it is, then," said Flo. "And you could try your hand at baking, if you like? Have you ever done any baking?"

Rob followed his son and his ex-girlfriend up to the house, unable to believe that his two worlds had collided and that the unbelievable had happened. The two people he most loved in the world liked each other.

5

_I_t was early. Too early for Rob. The sun was barely skimming the top of the hills, its tentative rays reaching the plateau upon which the cemetery stood, but not yet the town below.

He needed coffee. For the second morning running, he'd entered the kitchen at Belendroit to find Olly sitting fully dressed, on a chair at the table, reading a book, as if he were in a waiting room. Which was why, with an hour to spare before they were expected at Flo's, Rob had decided to show his son the final resting place of his mother.

It would be a beautiful day, Rob thought as he and Olly climbed to the top of the cemetery, which had fine views of the harbor and surrounding hills. But it wasn't the view he'd come to look at. He rested his hand on top of the marble white slab which gleamed as vividly in the early sun's rays as he remembered his mother had shone, and pointed to the name.

"This is your grandmother's grave, Olly. My mother's."

Olly's eyes widened. "Her body is under there?"

Rob nodded. "But I like to think of her how she was when

she was alive. She was always busy, laughing and the center of everything. We all loved her."

Olly looked thoughtfully at the headstone and traced a finger around the tracery of flowers engraved on it. "She sounds nice."

"She was. She'd have *loved* you."

"Is she with my mum?"

Rob hesitated. He couldn't imagine his mother and Cate, his ex, spending time together. They'd never met. His mother had died a few months before Cate and her family had arrived on holiday in Akaroa. They were like chalk and cheese. But he could hardly tell his son that.

"I reckon my mum will be looking after your mum, all right. She was big on nurturing, was my mum." Unlike his ex, thought Rob, keeping the thought to himself.

"Like Flo," said Olly, glancing across the town towards Flo's house, whose chimney pots were just catching the rising sun.

Rob couldn't speak for a few seconds, surprised that Olly should have made such a mature judgement about someone he hardly knew.

Olly looked up, obviously puzzled by Rob's lack of response. "I overheard you say to Grandad that Flo was a nurt...nurturer." He stumbled slightly over the word. "I looked it up. Someone who cares for other people."

"That's right. She is." To a fault, he felt like adding. He suspected part of the reason she focused so much on caring for others was to deflect interest from herself. People depending on Flo was exactly what she wanted. That way, she could hide her own vulnerabilities. Maybe only he and her closest friends knew they were there. But perhaps things were changing. At least they were getting along now, and she'd agreed that he could work on the house. He'd take it slowly, but he was determined to work things out with her.

He felt too much for her to let her slip through his fingers again.

Rob tapped the marble, smoothing his hands over it and squeezing it as if it were a shoulder. "Just thought I'd introduce you to Olly, Mum."

Olly looked up in surprise. "You talk to her?"

"Yep. I've been away too long and have a lot to tell her, so I come up here as often as I can. It's peaceful, and I feel close to her."

"That's nice."

"Yes, it is." Rob smiled at his son—so quirky yet, somehow, here he seemed to be in his element. He thought his son had more empathy and compassion for people than anyone else he knew. Except one. He glanced down again at his mother's grave. "You two would have got on so well."

Olly knelt down beside Rob and reached out and patted the marble headstone. "Hello, Grandma." He rolled back on his heels. "I wish I could do that with my mum."

Rob winced. "You know, when people pass away, they're not limited to a single place or time." He tapped his heart. "She's in there, a part of you for always."

Olly blinked and looked out across the harbor, his eyes far away. Rob's heart hurt for his son. But then Olly smiled and his brown eyes warmed, the color of chocolate. He pressed his chest in a vague approximation of his heart. "I think I can feel her." He jumped up. "It feels nice."

"Good. She loved you with all her heart."

Olly nodded. "And I loved her."

Below them, on a piece of land which jutted out into the still shadowy harbor, sat Belendroit, its lanterns bobbing in the morning breeze, still alight in the shady hours of early morning. "Why are there lanterns everywhere at Belendroit?"

"Because your grandma loved them. She reckoned they

always needed to be lit so that her children would find their way home. It was some kind of family tradition which began long before her."

"Has it worked?"

"I'm here, aren't I?"

"And so am I!" said Olly with a grin. He turned to the lighthouse which stood halfway between Flo's place and Belendroit. "But why isn't the lighthouse ever lit?"

"Because it's not in use anymore."

"So the light never shines?"

"It used to. Which reminds me. I have a meeting with someone so we'd best get off." Rob ruffled Olly's hair. "Come on, I'll take you to Flo's."

FLO WAS ALWAYS the first to rise in the house. There was too much to do to indulge in a lie-in. But, this morning, she only had a few guests staying and, after their late night, she didn't think she'd be seeing them before eight. Besides, it wasn't housework which was at the forefront of her mind as she entered the kitchen. She switched on the stove for the coffeepot, and opened the pantry door where she kept her key rings.

She'd been putting it off. She knew that. But with Rob identifying which keys would fit the lock, she knew she couldn't delay it any longer, no matter what she might find in the safe. Her stomach fluttered with nerves as she unhooked the heavy iron ring. What would she find there? Some damning secret which her grandmother had wanted hidden? Family jewels? Flo laughed at the thought. She could only ever remember her grandmother wearing a gold chain with a small cross, and her wedding ring—a simple plain gold band, made slender with age. Or maybe, it held money. Maybe, rather than secrets and damnation, the safe held hope for the future?

She clasped the keys firmly in her hand and closed the pantry door. More likely, it contained nothing. Most likely, her grandmother couldn't be bothered to pull out a safe which was no longer in use and merely papered over it. But why hadn't she ever said anything to Flo about it? Whatever, she had to check. Rob said he'd remove it for her by the end of today and fill the gap with wallboard to make wallpapering easier. She only had today, and Olly was due soon.

She poured herself a cup of coffee and took it into the dining room. She'd made more progress on the stripping of the wallpaper, and the old dark gunmetal gray safe was starkly revealed, two-thirds of the way up the wall, half-way between two fitted bookshelves. No doubt it would have always been covered by the oil painting which had hung there, even after the safe had been wallpapered over. The reason she'd never noticed its lumpy outline before.

She sipped her coffee and placed it on the workbench where her wallpapering tools were, and took the keys and advanced on the safe with a pounding heart. She fumbled and dropped them with a clatter on the bare floorboards— the rugs having been rolled up in the middle of the room. She took a deep breath. This was ridiculous! She pushed the first key, which Rob had suggested, into the lock. It went straight in. She wriggled it around and then twisted it away from the lock and the mechanism moved smoothly with a satisfying clunk and popped open.

Flo exhaled with a grunt, and stepped away, wiping her damp palm on her jeans. Now was the moment. It had opened easily, as if it had wanted to be opened. The notion gripped her as it released a dusty smell of paper and lavender. Ridiculous! But as she opened the door wide and peered in, she suddenly realized that the last time anyone had looked in here was in the 90s, presumably her grandmother. It was a strange thought, and she almost felt her grandmother's presence. It had always been reassuring, and she felt that reassurance now. It would be all right. She smiled to herself and relaxed as she reached in and withdrew a file. She checked the safe held nothing else then, taking the file and her coffee, stepped outside into the fresh morning air. The sun had risen over the hills and bathed the small courtyard at the side of the front garden in sunlight. Again, Flo felt reassured. She placed the coffee on the wrought-iron table and sat on the bench and opened the file.

The first thing she saw was 'COPY' stamped across the top. Whatever legal document this was—and she could see at a glance that it was some kind of legal document—another one was in existence. She scanned it but only took in that it was the Last Will and Testament of someone. She noticed her grandparents' names and the address of the house. She sat back, looked into the fresh blue sky, white fluffy clouds scudding overhead, and took another deep breath. Slowly, she told herself. Slowly.

She took another sip of the now lukewarm coffee and sat back and read the document from the beginning. With each paragraph, Flo's stomach knotted a little more. Her first glance had told her it was someone's Last Will and Testament. A closer reading told her it was her grandfather's. A number of re-reads of one particular paragraph told her she'd stumbled upon something which was worse than anything she'd anticipated. This was certainly no family jewels, no money. Neither was it a scandalous secret which would taint their family's reputation. She'd been reading too many novels, because the papers before her were far more everyday. There was nothing sensational about a Will. Everyone had one. But not everyone had one bequeathing everything—including the family home—to their son, who had deserted them over twenty years earlier.

Flo's hands shook as she dropped the papers on the bench. She jumped up, grabbed her coffee and paced the small patio. Her heart raced as the words jumbled in her brain, but the meaning spoke to her loud and clear. She paused and looked up at the house—its gray weatherboards gleaming and brick chimneys proud and handsome in the morning light—a house which she'd always considered hers. But it wasn't. Her grandfather had left it to her father—a man about whom she knew nothing and wanted to know even less. A man who hadn't only deserted his parents, but had abandoned her. *This* was the man who was the true owner of her house, her everything. Not her.

Suddenly she heard voices, and she saw that Rob and Olly had parked on the road at the front of the house without her noticing, so caught up was she in her find. Rob waved over the fence, but she couldn't see Olly as they made their way around to the back of the house, now that the stream had receded and the small bridge was accessible. But she could hear Olly quietly answering his father's questions.

Quickly, she gathered the papers, which had scattered along the bench. She pushed them back into the file, scrunching them slightly with hands made clumsy by panic. Once inside the house, she went directly back to the dining room, and thrust them into the safe and locked it quickly. Instinct told her to hide them, and to keep them hidden. If no one knew, then she would be all right.

But, despite that thought, she knew she was kidding herself. The papers had COPY stamped on them. That meant that someone else had a copy. But who? The lawyer? Her father? And how many copies were there in existence?

If she weren't so frightened and agitated, she would have

wept. It didn't seem to matter how hard she tried, everything kept being taken away from her.

"Flo!" called Rob, after a quick knock at the door. "Okay if we come in?"

Flo gripped her hands and drew in a ragged breath. She could do this. She could forget this ever happened.

"Sure! I'll be with you in a sec."

She did a quick check as she went to leave the room and saw the keys, evidence of the thing she wanted to cover up, of her guilt, sitting on the sideboard. Quickly, she grabbed them and went back into the hall, firmly closing the door behind her.

"Hey!" said Rob, his hand gripping Olly's. His smile faltered. "Is everything okay?" He glanced down at the keys she half-held behind her back. "Did you get it open?"

She made some kind of shrug, grimaced and looked down at Olly. "Hey there! How are you doing?"

"Good, thanks! That's what Dad says New Zealand people say."

She didn't look at Rob, but nodded seriously at Olly. "It is. Let's go into the kitchen, shall we? My guests will expect breakfast soon."

"Can I help?"

"Of course you can. But there's something we have to do first. Do you know what it is?"

"Have a cuppa?" he said with a grin.

"Exactly. It's our British and New Zealand shared heritage." She looked up at Rob as they walked into the kitchen. "Would you like to share in our heritage, too?"

"Would have loved to, but I have meetings all morning. But"—he cleared his throat—"I'll be back this afternoon to work on the dining room."

"Oh!" She colored, despite herself. "I thought your guys were going to do it."

"They were"—Rob shifted from one foot to another—"they were," he repeated. "But I decided they were better working on something else. And I'd help you out. If that's okay?"

"I'm glad of any help you can give me. But I don't want to put you out.

"You're not. I assure you, you're not."

She nodded. "Good. But, I wonder, would you mind working on something else? There's plenty to choose from," she said with a rueful grin.

"Sure," said Rob, frowning slightly. "But I thought we'd agreed we'd start there as it will be used for meetings, which bring in income."

"Yes, but tomorrow would be better. I just need to get that safe sorted."

He grunted, as if confused. "Of course. I'd have thought one of those keys fitted. If they didn't, let me know and I'll get a locksmith to open it for you."

"Thanks. I'll, er, let you know how I get on."

Rob's gaze moved from Flo to Olly. He grinned. "Enjoy yourself, Ol, and help Flo out wherever you can." He looked back at Flo. "Thanks, Flo, I really appreciate it."

"It's my pleasure. Olly is a great helper and also happens to be great company. I'll see you when I see you."

Olly ran outside to wave goodbye to his dad as he walked alongside the fence, but he didn't wait until he'd got into the car before he came back inside the kitchen. It was Flo who gave Rob a last wave.

As she set Olly to some tasks, filling the kettle and getting things out of the pantry for breakfast, Flo's mind strayed to her grandmother. Why did she hide the safe? She must have been able to open it with the key, just as Flo had done. Why not throw away the key? Why not throw away the documents? But she couldn't imagine her grandmother doing either. She had been a law-abiding citizen, a staunch conservative. She obviously hadn't liked, or approved of, her husband's will, but, equally, she hadn't wanted to destroy it. Just hide it. For a long time to come. Probably hoping that, when eventually it did surface, it would no longer be relevant. She remembered her grandmother always professing to love the wallpaper, even when Flo had suggested making a change. And Flo had unwittingly aided her grandmother's plan by leaving that room until the last to re-decorate. And now she knew why. Her house wasn't hers.

WITH HER GUESTS MOVED ON, and no one booked in for the next few days, Flo took the opportunity to postpone the baking she had to do for the café for a while and take Olly to the beach. It was a beautiful day, the sun bright and the brisk wind warm. Flo hadn't bothered to put on any shoes and was surprised when Ollie seemed reluctant to come with her.

"Don't you like the beach?"

"It's alright. I don't know. It's sort of mucky."

She put her hands on her hips. "Mucky?" She swallowed her instinctive laugh because she could see he was being serious. "It's just sand. Actually, sand is really clean when you think about it. Most of this is washed each night by the sea. And the rain sorts out the rest because it runs through the sand." She picked up a handful and let it drift through her fingers, showing him her hand at the end. "See, no muck. Just a salty sandiness."

He tentatively stood on the beach just outside her fence.

"Fancy a paddle?"

He shook his head vehemently.

"Okay, how about I show you the indentations in the ground over there which your Aunty Maddy told me were the homes of Maori centuries ago?"

His eyes brightened. She guessed that didn't sound as scary as paddling or digging holes in the sand.

After checking out the archaeological remains and recounting the stories of early settlers in the area, Flo had managed to coax Olly to take his shoes and socks off, which she considered a victory. And the time slipped by building a sand castle, enjoying a picnic lunch and talking to locals who all made a fuss of Olly. It wasn't until they walked further along the beach that she noticed Rob's four-wheel drive parked at the front of the house.

"Hey, it looks like your dad has come early and is working at the house." She stuck out a hand to him. "Shall we find out how he's getting on?"

Olly jumped up and Flo noticed him wipe his hands on his trousers, copying her, and she smiled. She'd make a kiwi kid out of him yet. "Sure, Flo." He didn't seek her hand this time, but walked along with all the confidence that had previously been missing.

As Flo raised the latch on her gate, Rob stood up and looked over the roof at them. He took off his cap and wiped his forehead. "Well, hello, you two. About time you stopped digging in the sand and came and gave a worker some refreshment."

"We weren't digging, Dad," said Olly, running around the house to the porch, where Rob was putting the finishing touches to a new porch roof.

"Then what were you doing?"

"Exploring. Like Aunty Maddy does at Belendroit."

"Hey, Rob," said Flo. "I didn't expect to see you until later."

"Yeah, well, my last meeting was cancelled, so I thought I'd finish off here."

She shaded her eyes against the sun which streamed over the roof. "You've got the roof on! That's amazing. It looks brilliant. I bet it hasn't looked like this since when it was first built."

"Why, thank you. Good to know I haven't lost my touch."

She turned to him and dropped her hand. He had a sheen of sweat on his forehead and was covered with sawdust on his checked shirt. A couple of buttons were open, revealing tanned skin and strands of chest hair, blonde against the rich brown of his skin. She had an overwhelming urge to touch his chest. Just once. Just to see whether he felt the same. He looked stronger than all those years ago when they'd been a couple. Broader, more muscly and much more determined. He was a different man, and she had to remember that. She clenched her hand into a fist and smiled.

"Would you like a beer before you go?"

"No thanks. I have plans for tonight." He turned to Olly. "Why don't you collect your things, as we need to make tracks?"

Her heart dropped, and she turned away to follow Olly inside. She'd thought that maybe, just maybe, Rob was enjoying being with her. But of course she was only a small part of his life, and a useful one. He was simply relieved that someone was looking after Olly.

Before she went inside, Rob jumped off the ladder and dipped his head so she had to face him.

"What's up?" he asked.

She stepped away. "Nothing. Nothing's up." She looked around and picked up some gardening gloves which Olly must have left outside. She put a foot on the step of the porch. "Why would there be?"

"Because you're on edge."

"Nonsense." She took another step up to the porch floor, bounced on it, and nodded to him in approval. "Doesn't just look good. It feels pretty sound, too."

"Of course it is. I'm not interested in disguising shoddy

work with pretty paint. If I do something, I do it right. I thought you'd know that." He gave a sexy grin. "I'm not interested in anything superficial."

She shot him another glance. She was confused. One minute he was acting cool, the next sounding mysterious enough to get her heart rate elevated. Something was going on and she hadn't a clue what. But she would.

"So where are you going tonight? Got a hot date?" she asked. May as well get to the point of things. She needed to know. She held her breath as his sexy grin got even sexier.

"Now, there's a personal question, if ever there was one."

"Sorry, you don't have to answer it." She pushed her hair to one side and tossed the gloves onto a chair, which he'd placed back outside the porch.

"Then why did you ask it?"

A flare of anger shot through her. She looked him directly in the eyes. "Because I was curious about what could be more important than having a beer with me on the newly built porch."

He grunted. "What could be more important? You think you're pretty important to me, do you?"

A blush bloomed on her face. "No, I don't think so." She gnawed her lip, wondering whether to tell him, but he'd got her backed into a corner and honesty was the only way out. "I'd hoped so."

His smile broadened. "If you come to dinner with me tonight, I'll tell you."

"Robert Connelly! Are you messing with me? Were you going to ask me to dinner all along?"

"Yes. So, what's your answer?"

"We could save money and I could cook for you."

"Now, that would be very nice, but it's not what I want. I've booked a table at St Augustine's."

"St Augustine's? But that will cost a fortune! We can discuss the work you're doing on the house just as well here."

He suddenly reached out and took both her hands in his. "Flo, listen to me. I'm not asking you to dinner at St Augustine's to discuss the work on the house. I'm asking you out on a date."

"A date," she whispered, her voice having been swallowed by her amazement.

"Yes, a date. Have you heard of one of those?"

She cleared her throat, trying to get a grip not just on the situation, but her own runaway thoughts. "Not in relation to me, I haven't."

"Then, it's about time you had." He brought her hands up and looked at them and she thought, for a moment, that he was about to kiss them. Then he seemed to think better of it, released them and stepped away. "I'll pick you up at seven thirty." He stepped inside. "Olly!" he called. "You ready?"

Olly's running footsteps could be heard along the hall and he appeared with his shoes in his hands, damp, sandy patches on his trousers and a happy, chocolate-smeared face.

Rob blinked and pressed his lips together and shot her a watery-eyed look of thanks, before ruffling Olly's head and putting his arm around him. He was about to say something to Olly, but Olly beat him to it.

"Thanks for having me, Flo. I've had fun."

"You're welcome. So have I."

Rob looked from one to the other. "I think I'd like some of that fun."

"Play your cards right," she found herself saying, "and you just might."

He laughed and walked off with Olly talking ten-to-the-dozen, oblivious to any undercurrents between Flo and Rob. But Flo wasn't.

At the fence, Rob turned around and waved before they disappeared through the gate and into his car.

What the hell had she done? She'd just said 'yes' to a date with Rob. Never in her wildest dreams had she imagined that happening. Well, maybe in her wildest dreams. Maybe she'd just have to create new wildest dreams. It didn't take her long, as she went humming up the stairs in search of something to wear.

6

*R*ob pulled up outside the restaurant, which sprawled along a ridge high above Akaroa, and switched off the engine. Flo peered up at its facade, studded with diamond-bright lights which shone out from large windows. It felt like a million miles—not one long winding car-ride—away from her world, which lay so far below them. Her heart sank.

She looked across at Rob, and her heart sank a little further. Dressed in a dark suit, white shirt and narrow tie, he looked every inch the business executive, which this restaurant welcomed with open arms. But would they welcome a slightly overweight woman whose clothing choices either made her look very dowdy or very sexy? She'd chosen sexy tonight but was beginning to think dowdy might have been a better choice. She'd drawn the line at showing her legs and had matched the lacy black top, made more modest with a black camisole, with black jeans. She plucked the stretchy lace away from her bust, but it pinged back in place. She sighed. She shouldn't have listened to Rachel and Amber.

"Well?" Rob asked.

"Well, what?"

"Are we going to sit here forever looking at each other, or are we going to eat? I'm starving."

She grinned. Here was the Rob she knew. "Eat. Definitely eat."

But, by the time Rob had got out of the car and held the door open for her, Flo was still wriggling in the seat, yanking up the top so it didn't reveal too much cleavage. What on earth had she been thinking when she'd agreed to wear the figure-hugging top which Rachel had chosen? But, even as she felt herself getting hot and bothered, she knew the answer. Because, unlike her usual baggy clothes, this top revealed her slender bits—namely her waist and arms. And that part of her which wanted to show off her slender bits to Rob had won over her sensible brain. Unfortunately, the Kardashian butt and bust were showcased for all to see.

She took a deep breath, swung both legs out and bounded up before Rob had a chance to see her cleavage on display. She shot him a bright smile and turned away to adjust her top. Unfortunately, she caught the eye of a man exiting the restaurant who grinned and looked her up and down. The man's grin quickly slipped as he caught Rob's dark look and he hurried over to his car.

"Who was that?" asked Rob, offering his arm. Her heart skipped a beat as she slid her hand through his arm.

"Who?"

"That man who was checking you out?"

She turned around to see the man in question driving out of the car park. "No idea. Maybe he mistook me for someone else."

Rob grunted. "He fancied you."

She laughed. "Of course he didn't. He was just being friendly." She turned to Rob, but he wasn't laughing. He still looked grumpy. She paused on the doorstep. "Why?" She poked him in the ribs. "You're acting like you're jealous! You're not, are you?"

"Of course not! I'm not the jealous type."

Flo felt rather deflated. There was some mysterious feminine part of her which she hadn't realized existed and which reveled in the idea of making a man jealous. Especially someone like Rob, who looked like he'd stepped out of a film. But he wasn't jealous. Not for the first time that night, or ever, she wondered why he'd asked her out.

"Right, of course you wouldn't be," she murmured as they entered the restaurant. While they stood for a few minutes waiting to be shown to their table, Flo tugged again at her top. Trouble was, if she wanted to hide her not-quite-flat stomach, her cleavage became exposed. She pulled it at the back to make sure it covered her butt.

"Why do you keep doing that?" Rob asked, looking behind her to see what was bothering her. "Have you got something caught up?"

"No!" She blushed. It didn't take much because she was feeling both embarrassed and hot. After looking around to make sure no one could overhear her, she went on tiptoes and whispered in his ear. "It's too tight." She rolled back onto her heels. "As my grandmother would have said, you can practically see what I ate for dinner last night."

He grinned. "It is most definitely *not* too tight. It's perfect. You look utterly gorgeous."

She felt hurt by the over-the-top, hopelessly inaccurate compliment. "Are you taking the mickey out of me? Because, if you are, please don't!"

"No, I'm not! Surely I can tell you that you look gorgeous, if you look gorgeous?"

"You can if I do, but I don't."

At that moment, the maitre d' greeted Rob effusively and asked them to follow him.

Flo had only ever been to the restaurant twice before, for wedding receptions. Then it had been acceptable to her, as it had been filled with family and friends. Now, as she followed the maitre d' to their table, she felt self-conscious as glamorous strangers cast inquisitive looks at her and Rob. And, to her further dismay, she realized they were dining in the center of the restaurant. There'd be no hiding away in the corner for her.

"Would you like a drink before dinner?" Rob asked Flo.

She shook her head. "Just water, please." She didn't think they'd stock the brand of beer she usually drank.

He leaned forward, crossed his arms on the snowy, stiffly starched tablecloth and stared at her. "Now, where were we?"

For a moment she felt like a rabbit caught in the headlights, unable to move, bewitched by his intense glare. She shook her head. "I don't know."

"Just as well I do. You were saying that you don't think you're gorgeous. Haven't you seen everyone in the room looking at you?"

She cast a surreptitious glance around. "They're probably wondering what on earth you're doing with me. Or maybe I've got something stuck to my teeth." She bared them at him. "Have I?"

"Hm," he said, peering at them. "Come closer."

She frowned, but did as he said. Then he reached over, tilted her chin and quickly, before she realized what he was doing, kissed her on the lips. She sat back in her chair with a start, her hand pressed against her lips.

"What are you doing?"

"Kissing you," he said calmly, sitting back in his chair and nodding for the smiling wine waiter to pour the drinks.

She couldn't say anything with the wine waiter close, so

contented herself with what she hoped was a glare. But the glare turned into a grin, which she could barely contain as he raised an eyebrow and his glass to her.

"Here's to an evening where, if you ask me a stupid question again, I'll have to kiss you again."

"It wasn't a stupid question. I haven't worn a top like this in forever."

"Then why now, if you feel uncomfortable? Don't tell me my sisters talked you into it."

"Well." She shrugged, embarrassed that she, a grown woman, had had a girlie afternoon with Rachel and Amber, first trawling through her limited wardrobe and then the local boutiques. "Not entirely. If they'd had their way, I'd be wearing a dress like Marilyn Monroe."

He gave a low, appreciative grunt. "I like the sound of that. You have a figure like Marilyn Monroe."

She spluttered into her water in a way that was very unlike Marilyn Monroe. "You're kidding me."

His face was dead serious. "I would never kid about something like your figure. It's a very serious matter, which requires very serious consideration." His lips tweaked in the corners. "And it's something I give a lot of thought to."

She cleared her throat and sat up tall. "Well, Rob, I think you shouldn't do that here. It's a public place and, well, you're leering at me."

He grunted a laugh. "I like to think of it as 'appreciating' you."

"You can call it what you like," she said primly, "but it's embarrassing me."

He nodded. "Fair enough. So tell me why you wanted to dress different to normal." She hesitated, not wanting to admit that she had, in fact, wanted him to look at her in exactly the way he had been. "So it wasn't my sisters..." He prompted.

"No. They certainly had input but, you know, in the end it was my decision. I..." She took a deep breath. "I wanted to look, you know, different for you."

He shrugged. "You're dressed up, but you don't look different. I think you'll always look the same to me."

"But I didn't want to look short, overweight and scruffy."

"You never look like that, mainly because you're *not* like that." He shrugged. "Maybe a little scruffy, but I don't mind that. And you work hard. It wouldn't be practical to do the work you do wearing dresses or a top like the one you're wearing now."

She followed his gaze down to her breasts. The weight of them had pulled the fabric down a little, revealing her generous cleavage. She hitched it back up again.

"Spoil sport," he said.

"Rob! You're doing it again!"

"I can't help it, Flo. You're gorgeous." He sighed. "Look, Flo, I realize I could tell you how amazing you look until I'm blue in the face and I doubt you'll believe me. So you're just going to have to take my word for it. You look amazing, sexy and beautiful, and I'm not teasing."

"Oh, okay then." She grinned. "I guess I could get used to you thinking I'm all of those things."

"I reckon it'll be harder for you to believe them yourself. You know what they say?"

"What?"

"Fake it until you make it."

"Maybe you're right. Maybe if I act beautiful, then I'll believe I am beautiful." She flicked her long hair back from her shoulders and leaned forward, cradling her glass of water as she looked at him in what she hoped was an alluring way.

He took her hand, and his eyes wrinkled at the corners as his warm gaze caressed her. "Flo, you really don't need to put on an act. It's in everything you do. Like your eyes. Has anyone ever told you that you have the most beautiful eyes?"

She sighed. "I could get used to this." She pressed her lips to her glass and took a sip of the luscious white wine which she hadn't even noticed being poured. His eyes dropped to her lips, and he shook his head.

"And your lips."

"Go on," she encouraged, swallowing the wine quickly.

He narrowed his eyes. "It's not just their fullness, but"—he reached over and with the tip of his forefinger swept around their outline, tickling her skin. She licked her lips and her tongue touched the tip of his finger. He sucked in a short breath, as if she'd taken a bite out of him. "*But*," he repeated, sitting back. "It's their shape, too." He shook his head. "I think we should stop this right now. You don't know what you're doing to me."

She grinned. "I might have an idea."

"Hold that idea until later tonight, after I escort you home."

"Rob!" Rob didn't turn around but Flo looked up to see a smiling Charlotte Kincaid descending on them, in a cloud of expensive perfume and a swish of sophisticated black, which revealed no flesh, only absolute class. Flo's smile dropped.

"And Flo!" Charlotte's voice pitched slightly higher in surprise.

"Charlotte," she said in greeting, taking another nervous sip of wine, while desperately wishing she hadn't chosen the type of outfit which made her look the opposite of sophisticated.

"I didn't expect to see you here," said Charlotte, looking at Flo, openly curious.

"Nor did I, until Rob asked me out a few hours ago."

The woman raised an eyebrow at Rob. "Really? So that's why you didn't want to meet up with me here."

A flicker of doubt passed through Flo. Had Rob really intended this to be a date, or had he been coming here anyway and changed it to a 'date' at the last minute to tease her? Rob shifted uncomfortably in his chair.

"I wonder if I might have a minute when you're free, Rob?" She turned to Flo. "I'm sure Flo won't mind."

"I think Flo will mind," replied Flo emphatically.

"I'm sorry, Charlotte," said Rob, after greeting her with a glancing kiss on her cheek. "But tonight isn't about business. Maybe we could catch up tomorrow?"

Charlotte's smile faltered and Flo felt unaccountably pleased. Flo smiled graciously at Charlotte. It was the least she could do, she thought smugly.

"Of course. Have a lovely evening and I'll see you tomorrow, Rob. Text me." She turned to Flo and shot her the sort of warm smile which only made Flo feel more inferior. "Enjoy your evening."

No doubt Charlotte meant her words to be taken at face value, but Flo's insecurities threw up other meanings. Like, enjoy it while it lasts, because Rob isn't going to hang around. He's far better than you.

She waited until Charlotte was out of sight. "What did she mean by that?"

He shrugged. "Probably that you should enjoy yourself. It's just what people say."

"Yes," hissed Flo. "But Charlotte Kincaid isn't people, is she?"

"Isn't she? Then what is she?"

"She's…" Flo shook her head. "She's…" In a realm of her own, she wanted to say. "She's not like me," was all she could say to Rob.

"Then that's her loss, isn't it?" He took hold of Flo's hand and looked questioningly into her eyes. "What is it?"

Flo sighed and shot him a quick smile. "What is it? It's me. Charlotte is nice. I like her. I really do."

"Say it again, and I'll believe you."

"I like her," she said in a quiet voice. "But… she's the epitome of class and beauty. I wish I was like that."

"I'm glad you're not."

She clicked her tongue in dismissal. "Seriously, Rob."

"I *am* being serious." He gripped her hands in his. "Flo, we've been friends a long while and you've always been there for everybody." He flicked his tongue around his lips. "Unless…"

"Unless?" she prompted.

"Unless someone, like me, wanted more from you. And then the iron curtain slams down. And you turn away, not wanting to be vulnerable. I get it. I really do. But you have to stop. Or else you're going to spend your whole life alone—terrified of giving yourself to anyone in case they misuse the privilege."

She opened her mouth to speak, but her mouth was suddenly dry, and she closed it again. She gave a quick smile, more like a grimace, and tried to pull her hands out of his. He held on briefly, but then let them slide away. He sat back in his chair.

"Do you really want to keep up your defenses, to stop anyone getting close to you, forever?"

"I have lots of close friends."

"But not lovers. Not someone you give yourself to."

"Do I really have to give the whole of myself to someone in order to love?"

He nodded. "I think you do. Or perhaps that's just how I see love." He shrugged. "You have to be you. But I hope that doesn't mean you're going to shut me out forever."

She rubbed her forehead with firm fingers, trying to control the throbbing which had sprung from nowhere. "I don't mean to, Rob. But I find it so hard. A habit of a lifetime, I guess."

"Lizzi thinks it's because your parents left you."

Flo sat up straight, not caring that her top wriggled down a little lower. "You've been talking to your big sister about me?"

"Yes. She doesn't come to Akaroa often and somehow it's easier as she doesn't know you like the others do. And she's been through the mill with her first husband. She's wise. She understands people."

"Hm," she grunted, taking another sip of wine.

"So, is she correct?"

The memory of her parents leaving in the night while she was up in the attic room flitted through her mind. Another memory, years later, of listening to her grandparents argue while her grandfather defended their son, Flo's father, and her grandmother condemned him with words which cast her rejection in concrete.

"Yes, she is. I know it." She shrugged. "But what can I do? It still seems a pretty sensible option. It stops me from getting hurt. Trouble is, Rob, my backing off when you needed me ended up with *you* getting hurt. With us both getting hurt. And I'm sorry about that."

Rob held her gaze without speaking for a few long seconds. "I'm back now. And I don't want the same thing to happen again. I'm back to stay. And I want to be with you. What do you say, Flo?"

Myriad words and replies floated in her head, but the one she wanted remained elusive. It seemed it was one thing knowing she kept her protective shields up nice and high, but it was entirely another to lower them—to make herself vulnerable to this handsome, sexy man who sat in front of her, looking far too gorgeous for her. She shrugged, hiding a lifetime of pain behind the gesture. "I'm sorry, Rob, it just feels too hard. I don't know if I can."

He shook his head and opened his mouth to speak but closed it again as his phone rang. "I'll... just take this call. I won't be long."

She watched him leave, answering his phone as he went. She turned back to the window, looking out, unseeing, at the magnificent view. She'd often looked up and admired the restaurant—all glass frontage and majestic setting—and wondered what her house looked like from there. But now she couldn't be bothered to search for it. She felt numb.

Rob was saying all the things she'd longed to hear. Things which she'd imagined him saying in her weakest moments. Things which she'd responded to quite differently in her imagination. She'd imagined herself opening up to him, telling him—in a direct, but dignified way—that she was sorry she hadn't been there for him before, hadn't told him she loved him, but that she hadn't been ready. But she was ready now. A warm embrace would lead to other things, and she'd fall asleep with a contented smile. That was how it had gone in her dreams. But it turned out her imagination was a long way off reality. And that terrified kernel of herself that she kept shielded by an iron fortress was still terrified, and still well defended. Was it always going to be that way? Surely she could open up to him now, make herself vulnerable? It was time to put her insecurities aside and risk rejections, risk feeling, risk everything because living the life she'd been doing up till now wasn't enough.

She could do this. She nodded to herself, slugged back the rest of her wine and sat up tall in her seat. She was ready. She heaved a sigh of relief and smiled to herself. It had been a long time coming, but she was ready. When Rob returned, she'd tell him what she knew he'd been hoping to hear. And what she needed to say if she was ever going to find the love which had eluded her, her whole life.

A peel of feminine laughter broke into her thoughts. The kind which Flo could never aspire to. Flo's laugh had been described as infectious, raucous, but never feminine. There it went again. Flo couldn't help herself. She turned to see whether the woman looked as feminine as her laugh promised.

Flo's smile fell. The woman did, indeed, look exactly like her laughter. It was Charlotte, sitting in a corner with Rob leaning over her, talking. Her friend had disappeared, and the two were alone. Whatever he was saying seemed to be amusing Charlotte far too much for Flo's liking. She felt an instant pang of jealousy. Only heightened when Rob leaned in a little closer to the woman who was everything that Flo wasn't.

The jealousy was immediately swamped by anger. How could he? After he'll he'd said to her, how could he turn right around and flirt with the very person who was liable to evoke the biggest feelings of inferiority? Charlotte had it all. Money, class, looks, and now she had Rob. But not for long.

But, by the time Flo reached the table, Rob had left, progressing only to the next table where he greeted someone else. What was this place? Some kind of club for him and people like him? Obviously not people like her and her friends, because she knew no one here except Rob and Charlotte.

She'd intended to join Rob and Charlotte's conversation, but, with Rob having moved on to a table of people who were strangers, Flo stopped by Charlotte's table.

Charlotte smiled up at Flo expectantly. "I hope everything is going well with your house?" Charlotte glanced at Rob. "Rob tells me it's taking quite a bit of his time."

Flo's heart sank a little. Rob and Charlotte had been

talking about her and about what he was doing at her place? What else had been saying? That she was a millstone around his neck? That he felt sorry for her?

"Yes, he's been helping me out. I hope that hasn't been inconveniencing you," she added, unable to stop the edge in her voice.

Charlotte smiled again. What was it with this woman? She radiated a warmth and confidence, which only vexed Flo more. Charlotte wasn't only beautiful, poised, successful and clever, but she was also warm and lovely. Damn! "It has, actually. Rob and I were working together on a project which has had to be put aside until he can find time."

Flo shrugged. "It's up to Rob how he spends his time."

"I'd be really grateful if you'd give us Rob for a little while. It shouldn't take long, and we really need to nail down the details of the event."

"And you can't do this without Rob?"

"No. He and I are working on a special project." Charlotte smiled again. How could a woman smile so much?

Flo shifted her weight from one weary leg to another. Really, she shouldn't have worn the heels. "What kind of special project? Or is that a secret from me, too?"

"Yes, it is actually. Not just from you, but from everyone. It's going to be the culmination of the festival and I really need a one-on-one with Rob."

I bet you do, thought Flo. But Flo's confidence was draining away by the second. Just looking at Rob as he spoke with the group at the next table, and then looking back at Charlotte, she suddenly felt a cold clunk in her heart. They were perfect together. Two perfect people, beautifully dressed, confident, articulate. What the hell kind of chance did she have?

She gave Charlotte a tight smile. "Sure," she said. "I'll leave you to it."

Charlotte's smile faltered. "You don't have to go. We won't take long."

"That's fine. I don't want to get in the way. I'll take a taxi home. Would you mind telling Rob?" No, Flo thought not, as she walked away without waiting for an answer.

Flo went and picked up her handbag from her table. There was still no sign of Rob. No doubt talking to yet another group of friends. Who'd have thought he had so many friends when he'd only just returned from overseas after so long away? But, of course, he was a Connelly and friendships seemed to come easily to them all. Lucky them, she thought, bitterly.

In the end, she didn't have to ask the receptionist to get her a taxi. There happened to be one there, having just dropped someone off. She waited to one side as the people paid for the taxi. She half-expected Rob to make an appearance as the minutes ticked by. She scanned the windows but couldn't see him. Her gaze rested on the door, but no one exited. The couple finished paying the taxi driver and went hand-in-hand up the steps into the restaurant.

"Ready, love?" asked the taxi driver.

"Sure," she said, getting into the back seat.

"Where to?"

"Akaroa Backpackers."

"Backpackers, you say? What, the mauve and white tumbledown place by the beach?"

"It's not tumbledown!"

He shrugged. "Sure. It's the Ritz," he mumbled, as he set the clock and they drove down the hill. Flo glanced once more at the door, but there was no sign of Rob. No doubt he was already pouring a glass of wine for Charlotte for their very important discussions, which were far too top secret for the likes of Flo to know about.

She leaned her head against the window, and looked

down at the lights of Akaroa. The sooner she returned to her world, the better. Because all this 'date' had done was to show her exactly how different her world was to Rob's. And how right she'd been to keep her defenses intact. It wouldn't happen again.

7

"You did what?" asked Amber, dropping the cutlery back into the tray with a clatter. Her eyebrows were drawn down into an uncharacteristic frown.

Flo shifted from one foot to another. It wasn't often that Amber got annoyed with her. Or that she got annoyed with anyone, for that matter.

"I walked out," mumbled Flo, taking a quick sip of the coffee Amber had passed to her as soon as she'd entered the café. Flo didn't usually go to Amber's café so early but, after a sleepless night, she needed to talk to someone.

Amber sighed heavily, shot her a disapproving look and walked to the kitchen door from behind which could be heard the thud of oven doors closing, mixers whirring and someone laughing. "Can you cover for me for five minutes?" Amber called out over the noise.

"Hey," said Flo, as Amber re-emerged. "I'm sorry to turn up out of the blue." She regretted her spur-of-the-moment decision to seek out her best friend for advice. Was she mad?

Her bestie also happened to be Rob's little sister. She would hardly be unbiased.

"It's okay, we're not busy and I have enough staff." Amber slid into the seat opposite Flo. "So, tell me why you walked out on my brother." Amber folded her arms neatly across the table and Flo suddenly felt intimidated—not her usual reaction to her oldest friend. But Amber's self-confidence had gone from strength to strength since her marriage to David, who adored the ground she walked on.

"Well, to begin with, there was the restaurant..." She trailed off. "You know what it's like," she said, trying to appeal to Amber's sympathetic side. "You told me about the time David took you there."

"It's an upmarket restaurant," said Amber in an unpromising, no-nonsense tone. "You knew that before you agreed to the date. That can't be the reason you walked out on Rob."

"Well, no, of course not. Not entirely." She nibbled her bottom lip. Could she really tell Amber how ridiculously jealous she'd been?

"Flo," said Amber, in a low warning tone.

Flo looked up at Amber and held her gaze. "Charlotte was there."

Amber sat back in the chair, her hands clasped lightly in front of her, as if she were interviewing someone, her expression serious. Flo didn't think she'd ever seen Amber less smiley. "Charlotte?"

"Kincaid. You know, Miss Perfect. The lawyer."

"Yes, I know Charlotte. She's lovely."

"You think everyone is lovely."

"Sure do. Even you."

"Ooh," said Flo. "That hurts."

"I don't mean anything by it. Except that Charlotte really is a lovely person. And if you weren't so intimidated by how she looks, you'd realize that, too."

Flo opened her mouth to remonstrate, but closed it again, realizing that Amber was right.

"You have to be honest with yourself, Flo, because, unless you are, you'll keep on sabotaging the good things in your life because of your fears."

"Fears?" repeated Flo weakly. She never thought of herself as a fearful woman.

"Fears," repeated Amber firmly. "You're afraid of loving Rob, and you used Charlotte as an excuse. No doubt you told yourself that you're not good enough, or some such nonsense like that."

"I... Well, maybe..."

Amber tutted and shook her head. "That's good." She rose, looked at Flo sternly for a moment before reaching over and giving her a big hug. When she pulled away, she clasped Flo's shoulders firmly. "Admit you have these fears, and you're on the road to losing them."

For once, Flo was speechless. Amber came across to everyone as an easygoing, airy-fairy hippy, but people under-estimated her at their peril. And it seemed even she had underestimated her.

"Am I right, or am I right?" said Amber, refusing to release her grip on Flo's shoulders.

"You're right," repeated Flo weakly.

Amber released her. "Good. Now, open up that big heart of yours and love the people who love you."

"Right, then," said Flo with a frown.

"Gotta get back to work," said Amber, returning to the counter where she took over from the waitress, loading a tray of freshly baked croissants into the display cabinet.

Flo sat for a moment longer, pressing her hand to her forehead as she felt the pressure of emotion mount. For a horrible moment, she thought she might burst into tears. Instead, she cleared her throat, slugged back the coffee and jumped up. She walked over to the exit and paused, looking at Amber, wondering how her friend had metamorphosed into such a wise woman without her noticing.

"How did you know?"

"Because I've been there," said Amber over her shoulder, immediately switching her attention to the waitress who was piling sandwiches onto a pink plate decorated with flowers. Like everything else in Amber's café, the crockery was pretty and decorative. She adjusted the display and then looked up at Flo with her usual warm expression. "It'll be all right, Flo, you'll see. It may be hard, but it *will* be all right."

The tears which had threatened Flo before now pricked savagely in her eyes. All she could do was nod and walk out the door.

FLO TOOK her time walking back to her house. She took the beach route, not wanting to bump in to any neighbors or friends who might want to hold a normal conversation with her. Because 'normal' was a long way from how she felt. She tried not to, but she kept checking her phone. She'd expected a call, or at least a text, something to show that Rob had at least missed her last night. But she'd received precisely nothing. But then, what did she expect? Did she imagine he'd be thrilled that she'd walked out on him?

Last night, she'd imagined that he would be relieved to hang out with Charlotte instead of her. But then last night she'd been consumed by jealousy, which had fed her insecurities. This morning, especially after listening to Amber, she just felt... silly. She'd over-reacted, plain and simple. She'd indulged her insecurities rather than do the much harder thing of opening up her heart to Rob.

She paused outside her house for a moment. It was her life, her everything. But, despite its grand lines and decorative features, it was looking increasingly shabby. Its facade—from the peeling paint to the rusty guttering—was no longer fit for purpose. Much like the defenses she'd erected around her heart.

She sighed and looked up as some of her visitors emerged from the upstairs bedrooms onto the deck. Time to take over from Etta, Rachel's daughter, who had started helping her out in the mornings before school. Time, like Amber said, to give her fears the same attention she gave her work.

As soon as breakfast was over and she had cleared up, she went outside and did her usual round of the garden, checking on the veggies, making a mental note of jobs she'd do later, and trying to stop thinking about the previous night. The date which had begun so well, and which she'd twisted into something very different. She could name the point at which things had taken a turn for the worse—when she'd refused to discuss her feelings. She'd pushed him away again, and away he'd gone.

She pulled up some weeds with unnecessary force and threw them aside. The rumble of an approaching car made her jump up and brush her hands on her jeans. She shielded her eyes and watched as the high black profile of Rob's car slid along the fence line and parked outside her gate.

She felt a sudden flutter of nerves. He was early. She turned away, not wanting him to see her standing, staring at him, as he came to drop off Olly. But it was too late. It would be worse being caught scurrying away. She walked up to the gate and opened it for him.

She swallowed. "Good morning!" she said, as cheerily as possible. Maybe pretending nothing had happened was the best strategy.

He glanced at her with a raised eyebrow and slammed his

car door shut. He walked directly up to her and she gripped the gate. She suddenly realized there was no sign of Olly.

She dipped her head to better see inside Rob's car, but it was empty. Then she glanced up and down the street. There was no sign of him.

"Where's Olly?"

Rob stood in the open gateway, his hands in his jeans' pockets, his expression grim.

"Dad's back home now and he's happy to look after him."

"Oh!" Flo glanced away, not wanting Rob to see how disappointed she was. She blinked and forced herself to face Rob again. She shot him a smile, which faded when faced with his impassive expression. "He could still have come here."

"I didn't want to trouble you."

"He's no trouble, you know that."

"I don't think I know anything about you anymore," said Rob grimly, fixing her with his intense gaze. The blue of his eyes was icy cold.

Her stomach clenched with distress. She swallowed hard. "Would you like to come inside and talk?"

"Why? Would it do any good?"

She shrugged. "What you said about not knowing anything about me, it sounded like it was the beginning of something you wanted to say."

"No, you're quite wrong. It's the end of something I wanted to say."

Her stomach plummeted further, and she rubbed her forehead in distress. "Then why did you come?"

"To let you know Olly wouldn't be coming. I didn't think you'd have turned your phone on. You don't usually." He glanced at it lying on the patio table. "Obviously I was wrong."

"I... was just checking for messages."

"Did you think I'd hound you? Hey? Did you think I'd send you messages asking if you were all right? If there was anything I could do?"

She opened her mouth to speak but didn't say anything because she had thought exactly that. And now she realized how stupid she'd been.

"Yeah, I thought as much. But you're a capable woman who does nothing on a whim. You had your reasons and I have to respect them, don't I?"

Without waiting for an answer, he turned away and retraced his steps to the car. Flo felt as if something was being torn away from her.

"Rob!" she shouted and ran out into the street after him. She stood on the pavement and called over the roof of the car as he opened the door. "Please, don't go like this."

"How would you like me to go? I didn't think you would be very fussy about how I came or went, or that you would care anything at all about it after last night. You couldn't wait to get away."

"It wasn't you. You have to believe me. It wasn't over you that I left."

"Oh, I know that."

She did a double-take. "You do?"

"Yes, Flo, it doesn't take the mind of a forensic scientist to know that you were scared off by a smart restaurant and a smart woman. It was *me* who wasn't so smart, though, wasn't it?" He didn't wait for a response. "I thought you were ready to join the rest of the world, but I was wrong. You *weren't* ready. And I'm not so sure you'll ever be ready."

Pain blasted into her heart, and she blinked back tears. "I'm sorry, Rob," she gulped. "I should have stayed. It was stupid of me."

"At last, a sensible thought from you."

"Don't rub it in."

"Why not? You're smart about everyone else in the world except yourself and your feelings."

"I know," she said, grabbing the observation like a lifeline to keep Rob there. She couldn't let him leave like this. If he went now, she might never get a chance to make amends. "It's true. I'm like Maddy's toddler. She has such a temper on her that if she doesn't get her way, she throws her toys out of the cot one by one, even her teddy who is her special toy she can't live without. Oh, Rob! *I* am that toddler." She folded her arms around her waist, trying hard to keep her voice from wobbling. "*You* are that special toy."

Their gazes held for a long moment before Rob spluttered with laughter. Annoyed with himself that his anger had been pierced and dissolved so easily, he hesitated a moment, and then slammed closed the door and came across to her.

"This can't go on, Flo. At some point you have to stop being scared."

She bit her lip and nodded, but he didn't seem to notice.

"Because you'll never be truly happy if you keep hiding from things, scared that they will hurt you, scared that they'll reject you, scared you'll lose something of yourself."

She nodded again. "You're right. I know you're right. I went back to my old, comfortable way of behaving last night and as soon as I left Charlotte at the table, I knew I'd done the wrong thing."

"Then why didn't you come back?"

"Because I was too damn proud. I didn't want to look any more of a fool than I did already."

He sighed. "I shouldn't have left you at the table and gone and spoken to her. It was too soon. I'm sorry."

"No, what you did was entirely normal. You can't keep making allowances for me. I'm going to have to work on this or else I know that the worst thing will happen to me."

"And that is?"

"Losing you again. And I can't risk that. I'll do anything not to risk that."

His face softened, and he sighed. "Flo Pelletier, what the hell am I going to do with you?" He shook his head.

She opened her arms wide. "Give me a hug?" she suggested.

He stepped into her arms and they hugged for a long moment before he withdrew, keeping hold of her arms. "You, Flo, are a great hugger. But I happen to know you're a great kisser, too."

She gripped his shirt and rolled on tiptoe and, without further ado, pressed her lips to his. He snaked his arms around her back and brought her tight against him as he captured her mouth in a kiss, which put any other thought out of her mind except that, for once, she was in the right place.

"Um," he said as he pulled away, as if he'd just savored something delicious. He looked into her eyes and must have seen the desire there, because she made no attempt to hide it. "Hold that thought." He glanced over her shoulder as a door slammed. "Your guests are still hanging around and we don't have time for what I intend to do to you."

Every part of her melted. "And what exactly is that?"

"Well," he said, thrusting his fingers into her hair and kissing her thoroughly again. "It's going to begin with a kiss because I feel starved of them. And then, maybe I'll check out other places to kiss you."

"That," she gulped, "is very forward of you."

"Oh, you're going to have to get used to me being forward from now on. I've had enough of holding back, hoping you'll step up to a new you. What I'm going to do, Flo, is reveal that new you to you, so you can no longer deny its existence."

"That sounds… interesting."

He stepped away from her and gripped the garden gate. "Not as interesting as what else I intend to do."

"This sounds as if it's all about you."

"You're wrong there. The action might be all on my part, but I can assure you the enjoyment will not be mine alone. I'll make sure of that."

It was all she could not to jump into his arms there and then. But he was right. It had to wait. Life came first. And that meant looking after her guests, and letting Rob go to work. It was only when he was about to get in the car that she remembered.

"Rob! I've got some friends coming over tonight for dinner. Will you come?"

"Sure, I'll come."

"There might be folk music," she warned with a laugh.

"Looks like I'm acquiring a taste for it again." His gaze flickered down to her lips before he sucked in a sharp breath and turned away. He clicked his key and the door opened. "See you later, Flo."

She leaned on the gate for support. Her legs felt wobbly, and that wasn't all that felt wobbly. She also felt elated. She'd been given another chance, and she was determined she wouldn't mess it up. She waved as he roared by, giving a toot of his horn for good measure. She didn't bother to wipe the grin off her face as she returned to the house to bake cakes for the café, but with her mind on supper. Maybe dinner with friends could be postponed for once.

It was dark by the time Rob parked the car outside Flo's place. It had been a long day filled with business meetings in Christchurch, made even longer by the thought of the evening ahead. He couldn't wait. Since his life had derailed, getting together again with Flo had seemed an impossible dream. But it hadn't stopped him from dreaming of it. And here, now, his dream was the closest it had got to becoming reality.

The slam of his car door rang out on the quiet street, which was deserted as the warmth of the day quickly faded into a cool spring evening. Or almost deserted. Rob did a double-take as a stranger appeared out of nowhere and ambled past. He couldn't see his features, but he was sure he'd seen him before, in the exact same spot. The stranger appeared intently focused on Flo's house. Rob followed his gaze to see what the man might have been looking at, but could see nothing untoward, except a once magnificent house, worn around the edges but a house which would be magnificent again—at least it would if he had anything to do with it. He looked around again, but the man had disappeared. Rob dismissed his concern. It was probably nothing. Just a passer-by curious about the recent work on the porch.

Instead of going through the front gate, he took the side path which led to the rear of the house, from where the sound of music came. Rob crossed the small bridge, stepped onto the sand, and paused for a few moments.

Flo's house held a special place in his heart. It had been his second home growing up, and it had the same private access onto the beach as Belendroit had. And, like his family home, it had always been full of people. Except Flo's were paying guests and friends. With her grandparents and mother passed on, and her father long since vanished overseas, Flo was alone in the world. *Was*, he said, emphasizing the word firmly to himself. Because he didn't intend her to be anymore.

He turned his back on the lulling splash and drag of the sea on the sandy beach and opened Flo's gate, which led into her back garden. He was early despite fitting in a meeting with Charlotte because he wanted to make sure everything was organized for the work they were doing together. He wanted no more clashes, no more misunderstandings, to interfere with what he had going with Flo. He had no more personal interest in Charlotte than she had in him. She was a professional through and through, and simply wanted everything to be ready on time for the Festival of Lights. And he'd promised her it would be. He was looking forward to working on that particular project himself.

He walked up the sandy steps of the porch, and frowned. The music was a little louder but there wasn't a sign of anyone else through the doors which were open onto the night.

He stepped inside and immediately identified the source of the strange flickering light which spilled outside, onto the rear deck. Candles. Everywhere. He normally associated candles with Amber. Even David indulged her fetish with candles over electric lights. But he had to admit, they looked good in this setting. With its lofty proportions and decorated with paintings and furniture and bits and pieces which would have been at home in an antique shop, the room looked cozy and inviting, with the shadows receding and enlarging as the candles flickered in the sea breeze.

He opened his mouth to call Flo, but resisted at the last moment, and smiled instead. She was up to something. And he suspected it was something he was going to enjoy.

He walked through the room, down the grand hallway and quietly opened the door to the kitchen. His smile widened. Flo was singing to the music while she stirred the fragrant contents of a pot on the stove. He sighed and leaned against the wall, soaking up the sight of her in the same sexy outfit she'd worn to the restaurant. She'd obviously decided to give the date thing another go. Good. He stayed where he was, drinking her in, filling his senses with her. He felt as if he'd been lost in the desert and deprived of water for years. She was his water and he couldn't get enough of her.

He pushed himself off the wall to go to her but was arrested by the sound of her voice as it swelled along with the music. To say it was soulful was an understatement. Her singing voice, like her speaking voice, was deeper than most women's and had a rich tone. It carried, too, and soon the soaring notes filled the room.

Tears pricked his eyes as the vibrations of her voice filled his body as if they were a physical thing. He didn't so much hear her sing, as *feel* her sing. Her tone seemed to give away everything that was her—heart and soul—things which she kept hidden, she now revealed. And it only made him more determined to uncover the real her, and to make her understand the release this would bring her.

The last note faded and she licked the spoon, turned around and yelped at the sight of him.

"You're early!"

"And you're on your own."

She tried to conceal her blush as she poured the sauce over the meat and opened up the oven. He knew for a fact that Flo rarely blushed and felt an unreasonably macho satisfaction in making the woman he most wanted in the world react in such an unusual way for her. He was going to make sure Flo blushed again and again before he was finished tonight.

"Flo," he said as she closed the oven door. She turned slowly to him and he reached out and took her hand and tugged her closer to him. "Where is everyone? I thought you were having friends over."

A smile twitched at her lips. "I was but I told them something had come up." She shrugged. "I don't know, I just thought that…"

Her words faded into nothing as he stepped closer to her

and pushed his fingers through her hair until he was holding her face close, cupped in his hands.

"Thought what?" he murmured, as he brushed his lips against hers.

"I don't know," she gasped.

"*I* know something," he whispered close to her ear. He was rewarded by another sharp intake of breath and an increased pulse which he felt as he slid his finger down her neck.

"What?" she asked in the huskiest, sexiest tone he'd ever heard.

"That you'd better put that dinner on low because we're going to be busy over the next few hours."

"Hours?" she whimpered. "That sounds impressive."

"It won't just *sound* impressive," he said, taking hold of her hand and leading her out of the kitchen and toward the stairs which would lead to her bedroom. "It will *feel* impressive. Because one way or another, prepare to be subjected to a barrage of feeling—both physical, mental and emotional. Because, Flo Pelletier, tonight, I am about to blast down all your barriers and show you what that feels like."

She stopped walking and he turned to face her, wondering if he'd got it wrong, if she didn't want to re-ignite their relationship. She put her arms around his neck and opened her mouth, but not to speak. She rose on tiptoes and kissed him, and in that moment, he knew she was ready.

---

8

*F*lo didn't think she'd ever forget a minute of what passed that night. She and Rob had been lovers as teenagers—something of which Rob's mother had disapproved and of which her grandmother knew nothing. But neither she nor Rob had felt there was anything wrong with knowing each other so intimately. Neither of them could have imagined the heartache which would lie ahead of them.

And here, now, as she lay on her side, watching the early morning light creep into the room through the uncurtained windows, she couldn't believe how different it felt. Before, it had been like an awakening from innocence, fresh and keen. Now, there was a depth to each touch, each caress, which hadn't been there all those years before. Now, they both knew how transient these feelings could be and how they were all the more precious for that. When you'd lost something and found it again, Flo mused, you treasured it all the more. You savored it with your mind, as well as your body.

She sighed as the pale gray light of dawn limned the outline of his shoulder, cheek and nose. With his wavy hair swept off his face, exposing his strong brow and cheekbones, he looked as if he were carved in alabaster, like a hero depicted by an Italian sculptor. She felt a flash of uneasiness at how unreal he looked and reached out to touch his cheek. She felt an overwhelming urge to ground herself in him once more. But before her fingertips could touch his skin, his eyes flickered open. He immediately turned to her and a slow grin spread over his face.

"Flo." He caught her hand in his and rolled over closer to her. "Were you about to strangle me in my sleep, or something?" he said, kissing the hand he still held.

Tingles ran down her arm and through her body. She sighed. "Or something," she said.

He shifted even closer until their bodies were touching. "Maybe you should try it while I'm awake."

"Maybe I should," she said. "Except I'll use my lips rather than my fingers." She kissed his cheek tenderly and withdrew. "There. That's what I wanted to do."

He narrowed his eyes with a smile. "Touch my cheek?"

She bit her lip and nodded. "I couldn't quite believe you were real."

"Ah, I see." He stroked her back, sending shivers of delight all around her body, before stopping suddenly. "Do you know? I can think of another way I can convince you I'm real."

She laughed as his hand roved more freely. "Is that right?"

"Indeed, it is." He grabbed her and rolled her onto her back, with him above her. "Am I real enough for you yet?"

She grinned and shook her head.

"Okay, then I'm just going to have to demonstrate more vigorously."

Her laughter turned into a gasp as he proceeded to do just that.

. . .

WHEN SHE NEXT AWOKE, it was she who was being watched. Rob sat on a chair by the window, looking across at her. Sunlight blasted into the room and she suddenly realized she had no covers over her. She yelped and pulled the duvet over her nakedness.

Rob laughed and stood up. "Too late for that. I've been studying your body for some time."

A deep blush shot through to the roots of her hair. She muttered a swear word under her breath as she grabbed her robe and quickly put it on, tying the knot tight for good measure. "*That* is not fair, Robert Connelly."

His grin widened. "It's also too late for formality. You'll have to face it, Flo," he said, tugging at the sash of her robe so it fell open. Quickly, before she could stop him, he slipped his hands around her naked waist. "I know what you look like, and I adore what you look like. You have an amazing body and I have no idea why you don't want to show it to the world. Although I'm glad you *don't* want to show it to the world. It's quite enough if you only show it to me."

He didn't give her time to reply before he showed her exactly how he felt as he pressed his lips to hers in a long and sensuous kiss.

"Um," he said eventually. "*And* you're an amazing kisser."

Her legs felt like jelly and she leaned into him, pressing her cheek against his beating heart. "I didn't realize how absolutely amazing I was."

"I know." He sounded more serious now, and she looked up and caught his gaze. He stroked her cheek. "And that's what last night was all about, or nearly all—trying to convince you how wonderful you are and how right we are for each other."

She frowned, and he shook his head and stepped away. "And if I didn't succeed, there's always tonight." He grinned and walked over to the bathroom. Flo couldn't take her eyes off him. He might be exaggerating about how gorgeous she was, but there was no doubting that the entire world would agree over his beauty.

He might not realize it, but he'd already convinced her that there was only one man for her.

ROB HADN'T STAYED for breakfast, as he wanted to be at Belendroit when Olly awoke. But, as Flo prepared breakfast for her backpacking guests, she didn't mind. She had plenty on her hands with her work, as well as the decorating, which had been neglected of late. Besides, she'd be seeing him in an hour when he came to drop Olly off. And then, after he'd finished his meetings in Christchurch, he'd be back. She knew it. And that knowledge had settled deep and safe inside of her.

The hour raced by and Flo was outside, hanging up the guests' towels on the washing line, when she heard his car pull up on the street outside her house. She went and opened the gate for them.

"Good morning, again," said Rob with a big grin. She blushed, but Olly didn't seem to notice as he greeted her, still exhibiting his trademark politeness, and disappeared into the kitchen where he knew a cup of hot chocolate would be waiting for him.

As soon as Olly had disappeared from view, Rob scooped Flo into his arms and kissed her deeply. Eventually he pulled away, too soon for Flo, who found her hands had gripped the crisp folds of his shirt as if she never wanted to let him go. She released her grip with a soft, embarrassed grunt.

"And good morning to you," she said. "What are your plans?"

"For today or the rest of my life?"

"Today," she blurted, not wanting a serious talk.

"Um," he said, "shame, I'm in the mood for talking long term."

"No!" she squeaked. "I mean, some other time, maybe."

He frowned and swept his thumbs over her cheeks, gently cradling her face. "There's no *maybe* about it. We're going to have to talk about it sometime, Flo."

"Yes, but we've only just, you know…" She trailed off, after a quick, guilty glance towards the kitchen where she could see Olly looking into the cupboard where she kept the marshmallows.

"I'm not going to rush you, Flo. Take your time. Just know that I'm not thinking of us in the short term."

"Dad! I've made you a hot chocolate!" Olly's shout saved Flo from answering. It was one thing to know Rob was the right man for her, but quite another to let down the defenses of her heart and home and allow someone to challenge her independence on both fronts.

Flo followed Rob inside the house, pausing at the entrance for a few moments to enjoy the sight of Rob pretending to enjoy the taste of the lukewarm, watery chocolate Olly had made for his dad.

"I think your dad might want some cake with that." She grinned at Rob, who was managing to disguise his grimace with a smile while making all the right noises. She knew Rob wouldn't risk Olly seeing him pull a face.

She opened the pantry and withdrew one of the old tins she'd inherited from her grandmother's days at the house. They were stacked inside the walk-in pantry, alongside shelves of preserves and home-made jams. She eased off the lid, her mouth watering at the smell of freshly baked chocolate cake.

"Chocolate today. Is a double helping of chocolate okay with you two?"

Olly nodded his head vigorously.

"So," said Rob, swilling the unwanted drink around in his hands. "How is the decorating going?"

She pulled a face. "Slowly."

"Did you manage to open the safe?"

She didn't reply immediately but gained herself time by hunting for the plates Olly had admired, which featured cozy scenes of rabbits dressed in Victorian clothes. He seemed to love the family tableaux of safety and security and she reckoned a slice of home-made cake would be perfect on it. Not just a double helping of chocolate, but of protection around this vulnerable boy. She also decided to give herself a slice as well. Eating might well be safer than talking. She took a bite and shrugged.

Rob shot her a warning look. He knew what she was doing. How come she couldn't ever get away with anything with Rob? But she knew the answer. He knew her too well.

While he was waiting for her to answer, he rose and opened the door to where the keys hung and held them up to her. "Was I right?"

She swallowed and sighed. "Yes, you were right, and yes, I opened it."

"And?"

"And?" She got up to take advantage of the fact Olly needed a paper towel to wipe the chocolate off his face. She tore a piece of the roll, wet it slightly and handed it to Olly, showing where he'd smeared the cake.

She jumped as she felt Rob's hand on her shoulder and a gentle squeeze. "And, Flo, what was inside it? It was obviously something important, otherwise you'd have told me."

She turned to him and took the keys from his hands. "I'll do better than tell you. I'll show you."

"I'll be back in a minute, Olly."

Leaving Olly to spread more chocolate over his face, hands, and the table, Rob followed Flo across the hallway and into the dining room. Her heart thudded, and she had to wipe her sweaty palm on her jeans to hold the keys securely. The key clicked easily this time, and the heavy door swung open. She took a deep breath and grasped the papers. She hesitated a moment as she wondered what on earth she was doing. She hadn't told a soul about these papers and yet here she was, about to show them to Rob. But they had been eating away at her, worrying her, and she knew it was time to tell someone, and who better than Rob?

She turned to face him. "These were all that were inside."

He frowned. "Papers? No family jewels, money, or anything that might be of use?"

"No, nothing. Only these." She folded her arms and stepped away.

He scanned the front cover, then flicked through the legal documents with the ease of someone accustomed to getting to the heart of the matter straight away. His frown deepened as he focused on her father's name. Then he looked up at her with a wide-eyed look of surprise. "Your father?"

She nodded. "Yep. So it appears."

"Your grandfather left everything to your father?"

She nodded again.

He swore under his breath and shook his head as he looked at her again. "That must have knocked you for six. I know how much all this means to you."

"Sure did. I'm guessing my grandmother didn't agree with Grandad, but it doesn't look as if it influenced him at all. Not from this document, anyway. I'm no expert, but it looks legal to me."

"What did your lawyer say?"

"Nothing. I haven't been to see her yet."

"You haven't seen Charlotte yet?" He waved the documents in front of her. "Flo! You need to get on to it. You need to find out the exact status of these documents. They might not have any standing anymore. I mean, your grandad died before your grandmother. Maybe your grandmother's will superseded his."

"It did, but it doesn't affect this. It was *his* family who owned the house, not my grandmother's. So he had every right to dispose of it as he saw fit. And, I guess Gran didn't approve and so hid it behind wallpaper."

"Hoping it wouldn't be discovered until it was no longer relevant," Rob added.

She shrugged. "And it might *well* not be relevant. No one has seen or heard from my dad for decades. If he's not dead, then he's obviously not interested in his family home, otherwise I'd have imagined he'd have contacted me, his daughter." She couldn't prevent the bitterness from creeping into her voice.

"Yeah, you're right. Of course you're right. Still, if I were you, I'd see Charlotte and verify its legality, at the very least."

"Yes, but then, it'll be known. And, if my father is alive, then he'd be within his rights to come here and take everything I've worked for, everything I have in the world, away from me. But if it stays here, no one will be any the wiser."

"Flo," he said gently. "You do know that it says 'copy' on it. You did see that, didn't you?"

She bit her lip and nodded.

"Then someone else already knows. And there's nothing you can do about it."

Flo was saved from replying by the strident ringtone of Rob's phone. Rob dropped the papers on the dining room table and walked out into the garden to take the call. Flo immediately scooped up the papers and locked them firmly back in the safe once more. There would be no meetings with Charlotte Kincaid to discuss these documents. For one thing, she couldn't afford the legal fees and, for another, they were only papers and irrelevant ones at that. As far as she was concerned she didn't have a father and her world was secure.

But, as she turned to walk away, Rob's words repeated in her head. *Someone else already knows*. The question was, who?

DESPITE THE SHADOW of the papers hanging over her, Flo enjoyed her day with Olly. Every day she spent with him, she noticed more changes in him. Some, she knew, were because of things they'd done together, things which were slowly building up a confidence in himself which he hadn't had before. And yet others were because of Rob and his family. She couldn't imagine anyone living with the Connelly family and not feeling loved. They were that kind of family. What was harder was being on the outside, looking in at that kind of love. But the connection with Olly was bringing her closer to them all, and it felt good.

"So," she said, as their afternoon was drawing to a close. She glanced at the kitchen clock and knew that Rob would be dropping by soon to collect Olly. "What shall we do next week?"

Olly's bright expression suddenly faded. "Nothing."

"Nothing?" She put her hands on her hips. "We've got to do something. Nothing is boring."

"No, I mean, I can't do anything with you next week."

"Oh," she said. "Why's that?"

"Because I have to go to school."

"School? I didn't think term started until the following week."

"It starts on Monday."

"I guess I'm out of the loop when it comes to school terms, and your dad didn't say anything about school to me."

"He probably forgot because he goes silly around you. I told him so and he just laughed."

Flo spluttered a half-laugh at the thought of Rob acting silly around her, which she liked, and the thought of Rob knowing his son had observed this. Which she liked even better. It was almost enough to make her forget Olly's fears, as her mind drifted off into a reverie which was definitely X-rated.

"Do you think I'll make friends there?"

"Hm?" she replied absentmindedly. "Sorry, what's that?"

"Do you think I'll make friends at school? Dad says I will, but I'm worried no one will like me. That they'll say I talk posh and I won't know how to play their games." He lifted his large puppy-dog eyes to her. "I didn't play games at home with Mum."

"Of course you'll make friends. Who wouldn't want to be friends with you? You're great! What you need to do is have a bit of a practice first. Do you see your cousins much? Like Rachel's daughter, Etta?"

His face lit up, and he nodded vigorously. "Etta is really cool."

"That she is." And she was a real handful, thought Flo, if only half the things Amber had relayed to her were true. "She helps me out in the mornings, before you arrive. I'll ask her to drop by Belendroit at the weekend so you can ask her about the kind of games boys your age play. She'd know—she used to be a real tomboy. She'll help you out. That kid has a big heart."

He frowned thoughtfully and nodded. "That's a good idea."

"Cool. And then after school you can help me out in the garden, if you'd like."

His face lit up and then the smile faded as suddenly as it had arrived. He sighed heavily. "I can't."

"Why not?"

"Dad said Grandad would pick me up."

"Oh!"

She spun away to hide her surprise and, she realized immediately, her disappointment. It hadn't been long, but she'd got used to Olly being around. More than got used, she forced herself to admit, as she gathered Olly's things together in readiness for Rob's arrival. She liked him being around. He fulfilled a need she'd never dared admit she had.

"Well, that will be nice for you." She forced herself to smile. Olly didn't need to know about Flo's weaknesses.

"No, it won't. I like being here with you. But Dad said I couldn't. That you weren't family."

Not family. It was like a well-aimed spike going into her heart. She was the girl who cared for everyone and who belonged to no one. "Yes, well, that much is true. But," she said, forcing the ache into the background. Olly needed more comforting than she did. "If your grandad is ever too busy, I'll be happy for you to come around here. I could use your help in the garden and in the kitchen. You've proved to be an excellent cook and gardener."

He grinned. "I'll tell Dad."

"Well," she said, too brightly. "You'd better wash your hands. Your dad will be here to pick you up soon." And she couldn't help wondering if it might be for the last time.

Flo continued to tidy the kitchen while Olly sat at the table coloring in an old-fashioned picture of a garden, complete with hollyhocks and a thatched-roof cottage, his tongue stuck out to one side as he concentrated on carefully keeping within the lines. But Flo was too busy with her own escalating thoughts to suggest to Olly that the world wouldn't end if he went outside the lines, as she'd done before. No, she was too busy trying to shore up a hole which Olly's news had spiked in her heart and which was in danger of growing. Somehow, Olly had slipped beneath her defenses and she'd let him in. But he wasn't her child, and he was being taken from her.

Stupid, she thought, snapping out the towels and folding them to put them in the airing cupboard later. She felt angry with herself for allowing a place for Olly to open in her heart. And, although she knew it to be unreasonable, felt angry with Rob for taking Olly away from her. By the time she heard Rob's car draw up, she knew for sure what she *would not* do. She would not bottle things up like she'd done in the past. She needed to talk it through with Rob if they were ever going to have a chance of a future together.

"Rob," she greeted him as he came in the kitchen door. She watched as his smile dropped.

"Flo," he said, with a frown. "You're looking a little stern."

"Am I? Well, yes." She forced herself to give him some kind of reassuring smile and walked across and looked over Olly's shoulder. "Cool coloring in, Olly. Why don't you finish up there and go outside and get those seedlings we potted to take back to your place?"

Olly looked up with a gap-toothed smile at Rob. "Flo is showing me how to grow veggies and I can take some home!"

"That's great. You can plant them in your grandma's kitchen garden." They both watched Olly run outside, and Rob turned to Flo with a grunt and a smile. "You've worked wonders with Olly."

She raised her eyebrows. "Me? I haven't done anything. I was just thinking that you Connellys must have worked some magic on him because he definitely seems a different boy to the one who turned up here only a week ago."

Rob slipped his hands around her waist and she could feel her resolve to have a serious talk with him fade. "It's you who have spent most time with him." He brushed his thumb across her lips and she took a sharp intake of breath as a thrill settled deep inside of her.

"Maybe." Was it her imagination or had her voice suddenly gone husky as if she were some kind of sex siren? "But he hasn't stopped talking about you all, especially you. *You*," she said, pressing the flat of her palm against his chest, "are something of a hero to him."

"Um," he groaned as she slipped a finger under his shirt and stroked his chest. "That's good. And I hope I'm a hero to you, too."

"Of course," she said, pressing her lips briefly to his chest and breathing him in. "Every heroine needs a hero."

"You, Flo," he said in a rumbling, deep voice which vibrated through her body, "would tempt a saint." He pulled away from her and walked to the door, where he could see Olly. "And I'm no saint. Now, tell me why you weren't looking so happy when I came in."

Flo returned to her world with a start. "I wondered when you were going to tell me I'm no longer needed."

"What do you mean?"

"Olly said he's going to school on Monday. He said that he won't need to come here anymore."

"That's true. I thought you'd be relieved. I mean, you've been great, and he's had fun, but I know it's a huge inconvenience for you."

"Not really. In fact, not at all. I mean, at first I wasn't so sure, but he's such a great kid and I love having him around."

"And he loves being here with you, but it's no longer necessary. He's starting school on Monday and Dad will look after him after school."

"Oh. That's good then." She licked her lips, her mind racing to think of something positive to say, something very different to how she felt. She shot him a weak smile. "Your dad will enjoy being with him."

"Flo Pelletier. What's going on? What is it you're not saying?"

She huffed a laugh. "I guess I can't hide much from you."

"Nope. I reckon I can read you like a book."

"Okay. I guess I felt upset to think that Olly wouldn't come here again. To be honest, Rob, I've grown really fond of him, and I shouldn't have because I'm not family." There she'd said it, despite the lump in her throat which felt like the size of a billiard ball.

The door suddenly flung open and Olly walked in, balancing half-a dozen small pots on a tray. Rob stepped forward. "Let me take that, Olly."

"I can show my cousin Aimee, can't I, Dad?"

"Of course you can." Rob turned to Flo. "Lizzi, Pete and Aimee are coming to Belendroit tonight. Olly hasn't met them yet.

"That will be fun, Olly. You can ask Aimee about the games she plays in school, too."

"Good idea," said Rob. "And we can practice them over the weekend." He turned to Flo. "Thanks again, Flo. Catch you later."

"See you, Flo!" shouted Olly as he launched himself at Rob, who caught him and swung him outside onto the garden path with Olly laughing and Flo left feeling bereft.

Neither of them turned around, so absorbed were they in each other—Olly talking and Rob giving him his full attention. Exactly as it should be, thought Flo sternly to herself. Still, her eyes felt gritty as she watched the car roar off down the road and disappear into the distance.

She closed the door and went immediately into the kitchen and cut another piece of the chocolate cake which she and Olly had made. Then she poured a large glass of red wine and took them outside to the deck, which looked out onto the beach.

There were a few people walking along, all different ages, some dipping in for a swim, others taking a shortcut from the shops to the houses. Life going on around her. As the weather picked up, so would her business and life would carry on as normal. With her helping people, being there for them, and always returning to her house by herself. Outside any family other than the one she'd made for herself from friends, waifs and strays. She'd helped Rob out with his son. She'd been there for them, just as she was there for everybody. Trouble was, she thought, sometimes she wanted someone to be there for her.

As she sat, sipping her wine and watching the people pass by, she felt an overriding sense of sadness that Rob hadn't responded to her admission that she was hurting because she wasn't part of the Connelly family and had no claims on the little boy who'd stolen her heart. It had taken a lot to acknowledge the truth to him, but she didn't know if it had even registered with him.

he next morning, Flo was up and about early as usual, making a start on painting the woodwork in the dining room. She couldn't begin the wallpapering until Rob had moved the safe. He'd promised to do that at the weekend sometime. At least that meant she'd get to see him at some point.

Her phone pinged, and she wiped her hands on a cloth before checking to see who the text was from. Amber. Nothing unusual there. She heard from Amber most days. But, as she scrolled down the message, she realized what was unusual was that it was an invitation to go to dinner at Belendroit that evening.

"Why?" she texted back. "What's going on?"

"Nothing :) Just family stuff."

"But I'm not family."

There was a pause, and the phone rang. It was Amber.

A flow of consciousness from Amber ensued about the meaning of family and how insulted Amber felt that Flo didn't feel a part of hers. By the time Flo had finished the call, she found she was not only going to dinner at Belendroit, but had somehow also agreed to go on a shopping trip to the local boutique with both Amber and Rachel. Apparently, a dress was in order. Flo shook her head in despair as she returned to her painting. She never wore a dress.

ROB SCUFFED the footpath with his foot, as he re-ran his last conversation with Flo in the light of what Amber had told him. His only excuse was that Olly had distracted him. But now he could identify the strange tone in Flo's voice as she'd told him how she'd felt. He couldn't identify it yesterday, and no wonder, she'd never used it before. It was the tone of Flo opening up a part of herself rather than bottling things up. And he'd been stupid enough to allow the moment to pass. He scanned the footpath, but there still wasn't any sign of her. He was determined she wouldn't leave Belendroit tonight without knowing exactly how she fitted into his family.

"Rob! What on earth has got into you? Come over here and make yourself useful instead of staring at the footpath. She won't come any more quickly because of that!" bellowed Jim Connelly.

Rob glanced around to see who else was aware of the fact that he was watching out for Flo. Everyone was staring at him—the men looked embarrassed, his sisters and sisters-in-law, knowing. He did what a good kiwi bloke would do and took a swig of his beer and looked up at the sky. "Looks like rain."

"Maybe you should pick Flo up then," said Amber, looking with concern at the darkening sky. "She's wearing a new summer dress."

"The one with peonies on it?" asked Rachel. "That's really pretty. I'm glad I could persuade her to buy it together with the plain white one. She has an amazing figure."

Rob couldn't argue with that, but what struck him was that his sisters were talking about Flo and a dress in the same sentence. "She bought a dress for tonight?"

"Course she did, mate," said Zane. "She's got you in her sights." Zane's grin quickly fled when Rachel gave him a sharp tap on his arm. "I was only saying that she's obviously got herself dolled up tonight for a reason."

Rachel shot Zane a filthy look and Zane resorted to Rob's trick and focused on his beer, whose label suddenly appeared very interesting. Rachel glanced at Rob, who was feeling more unsettled with each passing minute. But not in a bad way. His hopes soared at the thought of Flo dressing up. She rarely dressed up. Even when she'd come to the restaurant, she'd worn trousers—albeit a very sexy top and trousers. But a dress? That would be a first. He didn't remember her wearing a dress since... His thoughts trailed off as he caught sight of familiar-colored hair bobbing up above the bank which separated their beach of Lantern Bay from the rest of the harbor. He'd recognize her hair anywhere. It was a deep browny-red—auburn, Rachel had once described it as—and thick and luscious. When he'd been going out with her, he'd used to hold it in his hands and smooth his fingers down the long strands. At first she'd used to flick it away, unused to the intimacy. But, before long, she'd stilled her head and watched him as he played with her hair. And then the playing had led to other kinds of play. The kinds which still evoked feelings which had never been met by any of the other women he'd had relationships with. And, after his divorce, there had been a few.

He didn't take his eyes off her as she stepped out onto the beach of Lantern Bay and caught sight of him watching her. She didn't stumble, not his Flo, but walked with purpose towards him. Rachel was right. The dress looked amazing on her. But then, so did everything. For a long time after Flo, he couldn't figure out why women seemed to fuss so much about their appearance, wear so many different outfits, always on the lookout for more. But then he realized why. Flo was different. She didn't need to be more than she was. But this dress exposed a sensual side which she usually kept under wraps. It was button-through with a small collar, and fitted neatly around the bust and waist, accentuated by a narrow belt, falling away in folds to her calves.

He took another hasty swig of his beer to calm his heartbeat. He was glad she'd decided to reveal herself in all her splendor tonight. Maybe his plan might succeed.

The two cocker spaniels, Stanley and Boo, were the first ones to bound up to Flo, their barks quickly fading after a couple of pats from Flo. Rob thought he could benefit by a quick rub of the neck by Flo, too. It might quieten *him* down as well. Then she looked up and her green eyes hooked his, just as they always had, and, he imagined, just as they always would.

"Flo," he greeted her, with his usual brevity, which hid so much.

"Rob," she smiled. "Thanks for inviting me to dinner. Or, rather, thanks for asking Amber to invite me to dinner."

"Ah, well. I thought you wouldn't refuse Amber."

She cocked her head to one side in a way that was decidedly coquettish, and in a way he decidedly liked. "But you thought I might refuse *you*."

"Well, yes. I wasn't sure, really…" He trailed off, at a loss, and turned and walked alongside her, the spaniels announcing their arrival to the others who were trying, without success, to hide the fact they were watching them.

"Wasn't sure about what?" she asked.

"My family is all here and I know they can be full on."

"Ah, but I know them all. I almost feel like—" She stopped

talking abruptly and glanced at him, a faint flush on her cheeks.

"Like what?"

She shrugged. "Nothing."

"Flo," he said in mock warning. "You never say anything without meaning something. What were you going to say?"

"Just that... I almost feel like one of the family."

He could feel the grin spread across his face and made no attempt to hide his joy. "You are," he said softly, as they walked up the steps onto the wide veranda, cluttered with furniture, throws, cushions, books, discarded cardigans and shawls and, everywhere there was a space, plates of food, half-full glasses of wine and soft drinks.

His brother, Gabe, shot her a warm smile. "Hey, Flo. How are you?" It was the usual greeting but, coming from Gabe, Akaroa's doctor, it sounded like a query about her health. Or it seemed Flo had taken it that way because she sounded almost formal in her response. "Very well, thanks."

"Good. Call in any time if you want to chat."

A chat? About what? Rob frowned at the exchange but remembered that Gabe must be Flo's doctor, a thought he found vaguely unsettling. But no doubt Gabe was just being his usual warm, open self. His surgery was practically an open house for people with problems—health or otherwise. But he had no time to dwell on the exchange before Amber leapt up, as if she'd been restraining herself, and flung herself at Flo. She gave her a big hug and kissed her on the cheek, still holding her close.

"Flo, you're back where you belong."

Rob winced. It was early days, and he didn't want to frighten Flo off. Amber meant well, and he knew she loved Flo like a sister, but even so, he and Flo had some way to go before they were officially a couple again. Flo shot Rob a guarded glance before smiling at Amber.

"Don't jump the gun, honey," said Flo. "It's only dinner."

"Sorry," said Amber with a quick shrug, her smile not diminishing even a tiny bit, before putting her arm through Flo's and turning to everyone. "I think you know everyone here, don't you, Flo?"

Flo responded to the mass of greetings before turning to Laura. "I don't think we've met."

"Oh, right!" said Amber. "This is Laura, Max's wife. You must have seen her YouTube channel?"

"Yes, of course. I know you, Laura, but we haven't actually met before," she said.

Laura, wearing tight jeans, loose camisole, with long blonde hair and bright smile, looked like she'd stepped out of an ad for healthy living. But a few years earlier, Laura had had a near-death experience from which she was now completely recovered.

"Lovely to meet you, Flo. I've heard all about you." Laura gave Flo a warm hug before returning to sit on Max's lap. Jim Connelly and the rest of the family had grown used to Laura and Max's physical closeness. They hardly ever left each other's side and only needed one chair, and a single bed suited them just fine. Which, as Jim said with a shrug, made it easier to fit everyone else in the house. Despite their close-ness, they didn't seem in any rush to have children.

"I don't need to guess to figure out who from," said Flo.

Amber held up her hands in surrender. "Okay, it was me. I admit it. I love nothing more than to talk about my wonderful family." She shot down Flo's look. "And you are one of the family, whether you like it or not."

"I like it," said Flo. And, again, Rob felt a warmth flood his veins. Maybe he could bring the moment he'd planned forward.

"Excellent!" Jim Connelly said, standing to one side to allow Pete, Lizzi's husband, to join them.

Pete held up a bunch of bottles from his winery. "My new Prosecco, hot off the press. Or, rather, chilled from the barrel."

After Flo was also introduced to Pete, Rob led Flo to a wicker chair, and sat beside her.

As Rachel appeared from the kitchen holding aloft a tray of nibbles straight from the oven, everyone dived on them, and Rob took the opportunity of leaning closer to Flo.

"You look beautiful."

Flo blushed, and Rob almost laughed. Flo's blushes were becoming less rare. "It's the dress," mumbled Flo. "I don't know why I agreed to go shopping with Amber and Rachel. I had no idea they were going to do something like this. Rachel bought it for me, you know."

Rob looked up just as Rachel shot an approving glance at them, and he smiled his thanks to her. After a difficult few years, Rachel was now reunited with her birth daughter Etta, happily married to Zane and had children of their own. And he could see her happiness alight in her eyes. Like most happily married people, she couldn't wait for others to be happily in love, too.

He turned back to Flo. "No, I didn't know, but I'm not surprised. It's the sort of thing Rachel would do. But, you know, she needn't have."

Flo stopped short from taking a sip, the wine glass hovering by her lips. "Why?"

"Because you always look beautiful. The best thing about this dress is that it shows me it matters what…" He hesitated, but decided to plough on. It was a time for honesty. Without it, they didn't stand a chance. "What other people think."

She shook her head. "You're part right and part wrong. It matters what *you* think."

Under the table, he took her hand and squeezed it. "Good."

Before he could say anymore, Etta gave Olly a push—which he didn't seem to mind—and he stumbled on to the deck.

"Are you all right?" asked Amber, full of motherly concern.

"Course he's all right," said Etta in her clear-as-a-bell voice. "Aren't you, mate?"

"Yes, Etta," Ollie replied with a trusting smile. It was obvious from day one that Olly had very much taken to his big cousin with her boyish ways and commanding air. She took no nonsense from anyone, but always respected her uncle, now step-father, Zane's authority. Which was just as well because, without it, no one knew where Etta's boundaries might lie. Rob suspected she didn't have any.

"Dinner is served in the dining room!" repeated Olly, louder this time. His pale face was bright red with a mixture of pride and embarrassment. Rob and Flo exchanged grins. Olly had come a long way since he'd first arrived in New Zealand.

"Ooh," said Etta, ruffling up Olly's slicked down hair. "You sound so posh and English."

"I won't soon, Etta," said Olly, lifting his serious face to hers. "Dad says I'll sound like a real kiwi soon."

"Ha! That will be the day," said Etta, munching on something Olly had baked. "But I'll let you off. You cook real good. Nearly as good as Mum," she said, shooting Rachel a big grin.

Rob stood up and offered his arm to Flo. For a moment he thought that his instinctive, old-fashioned gesture might be ignored, but Flo rose, her dress falling in folds softly around her, and smiled. She slipped her arm through his. He waited until everyone had gone through into the house and they were alone.

He shifted around so he was facing her and lifted her face. He wanted to see her clearly, and what he saw in her face didn't disappoint. He had so much he wanted to say to her, but words eluded him. Instead, he lifted her chin and dipped down and brushed his lips against hers.

"Thank you for coming."

He dropped his hand and found hers and squeezed it. "I wouldn't have missed it for the world," Flo said.

They walked into the house, and Rob thought he'd never been so happy.

FLO COULD HARDLY TAKE her eyes off Rob. He had been seated opposite her, for which she thanked Rachel. He was so handsome. Like Max, he was tall with a broad physique, and facially he looked like Gabe, but that was where the resemblance ended. He was much quieter, less gregarious than Gabe. She sighed. She could look at Rob all night.

It was only after a shout from Amber that she realized someone was talking to her. She looked at Amber, who grinned. "Dad's trying to get your attention."

"Sorry, Jim."

"I was saying how glad I am that the Festival of the Lights committee will be meeting back at your house again."

"Me, too."

"It sounds like it's going to be a really good festival," said Rob. "Charlotte was telling me the other day about some of the things they have planned."

At the mention of Charlotte's name, Flo's smile dropped a little. She couldn't seem to get away from Miss Perfect.

"Good timing, it being ten years since Mum passed away," said Max. Laura shot him a smile full of love and briefly leaned her head against his shoulder. Rob had told Flo that Max, being the eldest, had taken their mother's death very hard. Rob had never gotten to the bottom of it but, around the same time, a rift between Max and Jim had grown which, in no small part thanks to Laura, had now been well and truly healed.

Rachel's fork slipped from her fingers onto her plate with a clatter, and Zane put his arm around her. Silence fell over the group. Flo had known Mrs. Connelly and understood the spell which she'd created over her family—a spell which hadn't diminished over the years.

"It only seems like yesterday when she was with us," said Jim, pushing away his plate. "I'm glad we were all with her when she passed. Except Jonny, of course." He sighed heavily.

Rob turned to look out through the window, across the bay towards Akaroa. "It was the last time the lighthouse worked," he said. "I remember after all the rest of the festivities had faded away, only Mum's lanterns kept shining and the beam from the lighthouse kept swinging around. Mum was entranced by it."

"Shame it's not going any longer," said Zane. "We can't seem to get the correct parts to fix it. It was good for Akaroa, too. A real landmark." He turned to Flo. "Being close to your house, it would have been good publicity for your business, too."

Flo nodded. She picked up on Zane's attempt to divert the group. "And my business needs all the help it can get."

"Yes," said Jim, "I was concerned when I heard the committee was considering not meeting at your place anymore. That they were contemplating using the community center."

"Were?" Flo said. "Still are, I think. I'm hoping that the renovation work I'm doing will be enough. I need that income. Without it, I might have to sell the house."

"Sell?" Jim's shaggy white eyebrows rose in alarm. "Goodness, I hope not. What does your father think about that?"

Flo stilled instantly, and a feeling of nausea swamped her.

People continued to talk, but Rob also dropped his fork with a clatter at her stunned look. She licked her lips. Perhaps she'd misheard.

"I'm sorry. What did you say about my father?"

Jim looked at her as he chewed his food, suddenly wondering if he'd said something wrong. "Just wondered what your father would think about selling the house."

"I don't know. I haven't seen him in years. He was last heard of in Ecuador. That was when my mother died."

Jim frowned. "You haven't heard from him since?"

"No." One by one, the others at the table fell silent and looked at Flo. "Why, have you?"

He nodded. "It was some time ago. Through Lizzi." He indicated Lizzi, who looked startled at her unexpected involvement. "When Lizzi got me started with Facebook a few months ago. She reckoned I'd enjoy hunting down old friends and catching up with the news. Well, I did for a few days. Found a number of people and became their friends, including your father. Although I say 'became friends', we were friends for years before he left New Zealand."

"Dad!" said Rachel, looking anxiously from Flo to her father. "Tell us about Flo's father."

"We became friends on Facebook and exchanged a few words about the old days. Not much because after a few days I somehow got logged out and I couldn't remember my password."

"But what did he say?" asked Rachel.

"Not much, as I said. Just asked after me. I told him about my knee op, but that was about it."

"What about Flo?" asked Rob.

Jim's shaggy white brows lowered over his eyes in a deep frown. "He didn't mention her. I just assumed that you two were already in contact. Aren't you?"

Flo shook her head. "Did he say where he was?" Maybe he

was still in Ecuador, or some other far-flung place where she remained a distant figure in his mind. But then why was he enquiring after Jim Connelly's health, and not hers?

"Well, no, he didn't say."

Flo sighed and leaned back in her seat, the nausea only increasing.

"You've no idea?" pressed Rob.

"Yes, of course I have. He didn't have to tell me, because it was written in black and white, under his name."

"Where, for the love of God?" asked Rob, standing up.

"Christchurch. Ian Pelletier is in Christchurch. At least that what his Facebook profile said."

The shock hit Flo like a bomb blast, and for a minute she looked down at her hands, gripped together in her lap, surprised to see herself in one piece. She felt shattered. She took one agonized look at Rob and found she was standing unsteadily. She gripped the table.

Rachel jumped up and put her arm around her. "Are you all right? You look as if you've seen a ghost."

Flo turned to Rachel. "I haven't seen him, but he's a ghost all right. A ghost I thought I'd lost touch with, and who lived far away and had no interest in anything to do with home. Seems I was wrong on that score. The only thing he's not interested in is me."

She stepped back and her chair tipped over, falling with a sharp crack on the wooden floor. "I'm sorry." She pushed her hair off her face and looked around in a daze. "I have to go."

"Of course you do," said Rachel, shooting Rob a look laden with meaning. But Rob looked as shocked as Flo. He rose, said a few words to Olly, and then came over to her.

"Are you sure, Flo?"

She nodded. At the door, she turned to everyone. "Thank you for a lovely evening. I'm sorry, I…" She couldn't finish her sentence as she felt tears spring and a sob rise in her throat. With a strangled sound, she stumbled out into the hallway, and went through the already open door, down the steps onto the back lawn which led to the beach.

"Flo!" called Rob, running after her. "Let me run you home."

"No, I'll go the way I came."

He gave a frustrated grunt. "You're a stubborn woman, Flo."

She rounded on him, thankful for the anger which sprang up and obliterated the pain and grief, which had come out of nowhere at the knowledge that her father lived close by and had not tried to see her. Or even ask about her.

"I've had to be stubborn, Rob! It's all very well for you with such a lovely big family who cares for each other. I've not had one of those, which means I have to look after myself. And, if there's one thing I'm good at, it's looking after myself."

She turned to go again, but this time he placed his hand on her arm.

"And I'm trying to look after you, too. You're not alone anymore. I'm here now. You know you mean a lot to me, and I want to help."

The anger dissipated a little. "I know and you mean a lot to me, too, and I love that you've helped me so much. For the first time in forever, I haven't felt alone. But, now, I do." She blinked and pulled away from him. "I have to go and I have to go alone. I'm sorry, Rob."

"Flo. Don't do this. Don't push me away like this. I want to help."

"How can you? My parents rejected me and no matter what excuses have been invented to explain their disappearance from my life, they went away and never came back. Until now, and he doesn't even bother to get in touch. But do you know what worries me most?"

Rob shook his head.

"It's my house. My garden. My home. It's all I've ever had to rely on. If my father's back, then maybe none of it is mine anymore." She took a few steps. "Please apologize to the others. It's been a lovely evening, one of the best."

Blindly, she stumbled away, ducking under the lanterns which swung from the trees in the quickening breeze. Soon she'd left the lights of Lantern Bay and Belendroit behind her. Only when she'd passed the lighthouse, did she look across the water to her house. It lay in darkness—she had no guests tonight—and for the first time ever she looked at it as a stranger would, feeling the emotional gap between her and the house widen. Was it hers still, or did her father—who had long since deserted the place—consider himself to be its legal owner? And, if he was, where did that leave her?

10

Flo frowned at her phone. It was a hand-me-down which Maddy had given her when Maddy had discovered Flo was still using an old flip phone, which must have been over ten years old. But that had been two years ago and, with the amount of times Flo had dropped the darn thing on the hard wooden tiles in her kitchen, or had left it in the garden overnight, it had definitely seen better days.

Flo pressed the buttons again, but still she couldn't find the icon she'd been told to look for.

"What are you doing?" asked Maddy, as Flo pressed buttons randomly, her hand tensing around it as she didn't get the required result.

Flo jumped up and thrust it at Maddy. "Trying to find Facebook. Or Bookface, as your dad called it."

"Ah," said Maddy, an annoyingly understanding smile spreading across her face. "By the looks of things, you've run out of memory to download the app." She looked up at Flo as she paced the room, to ease her frustration. "You need a new phone."

"I can't afford one," Flo snapped. She held up her hand in apology. "I'm sorry. I'm on edge. I can never seem to afford anything. All I do is exist on the handouts from my friends, and now it seems my father is back, and the one thing I've always treasured, always thought of as mine"—she blinked back the tears—"may not be mine after all."

Maddy placed Flo's phone on the table and gave her a big hug. Maddy—a cool, Scandinavian blonde—had been reserved when she'd first come to New Zealand, but now, after being subjected to the hugs of the Connelly family, and especially the intimate hugs of her husband, Gabe Connelly, Maddy had become far more demonstrative.

She pulled away and Maddy's expression of sympathy was almost enough to make Flo's teariness surface again. But Flo refused to show her weakness in front of her friends, or anyone, come to that. She stepped out of Maddy's embrace. "I'm fine. Sorry, a moment of self-pity."

"Everyone's allowed a moment of self-pity. Or even a few moments. You don't have to be strong all the time."

"Yes, I do. Because if I'm not strong, I'll go under. There's no one to catch me."

Maddy bit her lip, hesitating a moment and then looked decisive. "We'd all catch you, you must know that. Especially Rob. He wouldn't hesitate."

Instinctively, Flo framed the words to deny it, to joke about it, to change the subject. But the words died on her lips and she gave a deep sigh instead.

"It's not that easy. Rob might want to catch me but, after he's caught me, would he want me?"

Maddy's beautiful face screwed up into an incredulous frown. "What are you talking about? Of course he would. Why wouldn't he? It's not as if he doesn't know you well. It's not as if this is a rushed thing. Gabe tells me that Rob was madly in love with you as a teenager. It was only their mum's death which put everything out of kilter."

"Out of kilter. That's a good expression. Kind of describes it perfectly, really, doesn't it? I guess time gives us a sense of perspective which we had no clue about while we were living it."

"Exactly." Maddy took hold of Flo's hands, as much, Flo suspected, to ensure she didn't walk away as to convey sympathy. "So, why not accept Rob's advances now?"

"Because, Maddy," said Flo, pulling her hands out of Maddy's and walking to the stove where a tray of blueberry muffins needed to be pulled out of the oven, "I'm not the same girl Rob knew all those years ago."

"What?"

Flo waved her hand dismissively. "It doesn't matter. It is what it is."

"But what *is* it?"

"Things change. People change. Anyway," she said, taking the hot tray from the oven. "What am I going to do about my father?"

As Maddy pulled out her own phone, Flo knew that this change of subject would work with Maddy. Maddy had an analytical brain which loved nothing more than a problem to solve and Maddy was straight on to it, pulling forth a large phone which wouldn't have looked out of place in Star Trek.

Flo slid the tray onto the table and peered over Maddy's shoulder.

"What on earth is that? It looks like something out of a sci-fi movie." Maddy shot Flo a disbelieving look and shook her head. "Admittedly, it is the latest—I can't resist techie gadgets—but it's not sci-fi stuff. It's contemporary, current stuff. You really—"

"Don't say it!" warned Flo, retreating to her tray of

muffins. She understood baking, and she understood people. "I know what I'm good at and I'll stick to it."

Maddy smiled. "And thank goodness for that. If the world was full of people like me, we'd never eat or talk to each other."

Flo laughed because Maddy was spot on. Maddy had to be the quietest person she knew, especially with strangers. She raised an inquisitive eyebrow at her.

"But you can track down stray fathers with your hi-tech, I take it?"

Maddy's blonde hair stayed in a curtain around her face as she focused on the screen in her hands, her fingers moving quickly. "Sure can." Her finger stopped scrolling. "Oh, that's so cute. Look–"

Flo squinted at the screen. "That's Olly and Jim."

"Yeah, in the garden at Belendroit. I couldn't help myself and videoed it." She turned up the volume. "Here, listen to what they're saying."

Flo listened as Olly told Jim how much he'd prefer to go to Flo's after school because his dad says she's the best.

Maddy laughed, saving Flo from having to find something to say which she couldn't—she was speechless—and took back the phone. "Couldn't resist showing you that. That came after Olly had been telling Jim the names of the herbs in the garden, names which you'd taught him. You've made a hit with that young man."

Flo swallowed. "He's cool."

"Like his dad." Maddy grinned. "Anyway, give me a minute and I'll see what I can find."

"I'll give you more than a minute," said Flo, sliding a plate with a muffin and a generous helping of butter across the table to Maddy, before putting on a fresh pot of coffee.

In the end it only took five minutes, during which Maddy

asked a few questions, before Maddy held her phone aloft with a triumphant smile. "Ta-da! I think I've found him."

Flo shook her head and brought two cups of coffee to the table and slid into the chair beside Maddy. "I don't believe it. You've done in five minutes what I haven't been able to do in over twenty years."

"Well, that's possibly because you haven't really tried."

Flo took a sip of her coffee and shrugged. "Grandad wrote a few letters, but after he died, Gran gave up in disgust. And then, after Gran passed away, I found the last address Grandad had for my parents and wrote to them, letting them know about Gran's death. I never heard anything."

"Don't you want to see?" Maddy held up her phone, obviously surprised that Flo hadn't grabbed the phone off her immediately. But there was a part of Flo that didn't want to see. Didn't want to admit that it was true, that her father was around and could come by anytime and claim his inheritance.

"I guess so."

Maddy turned the screen to Flo. "That's him. Well, it's someone with his name. Do you recognize him?"

Flo took a deep breath and peered at the photo. It was of a man in profile, looking out to a range of snow-topped mountains. The little she could see of his face showed it to be very tanned, weathered almost, as if he'd spent a lifetime outdoors. His hair was like hers, except there was less of it. She shrugged. "Haven't a clue. It could be anyone."

"Well, it's someone who has the same name as your dad."

"I guess there could be any number of people with the name of Ian Pelletier."

"Yeah, right," said Maddy facetiously. "Pelletier is such a common kiwi name."

"It's French and there are quite a few French names in Akaroa, descendants of the first settlers."

"And how many other Pelletiers are there?"

Flo sighed. "None."

"And would all these other Ian Pelletiers in New Zealand also be friends with Jim?" Maddy glanced at the phone. "Jim only just started on Facebook. But it looks like he's found a few people, including this man. Jim must have known it was him by either his appearance or by something he said. I can't see they've exchanged anything we can access, but maybe they used Messenger. And he seemed pretty certain that it was him last night at dinner. Sounds like they talked about the old days. Flo, it really does look like this is your man. Or your dad."

Flo bit her lip and studied the man who might be her father. Was it him? And why, after so long running around the world, avoiding his family and the place of his birth, did he accept an old friend's Facebook request? Or even *be* on Facebook in the first place? That bit didn't add up. But then, little about her father added up. Suddenly, a frisson of fear shuddered through her, leaving her feeling cold and empty. She looked up at Maddy.

"What should I do, Maddy?"

Maddy placed a hand on her friend's shoulder. "I don't think I've ever known you ask for advice before."

"That's because I haven't. But this stumps me. I'm out of my depth here and the consequences of making the wrong move are too huge for me to contemplate."

"You've always taken control of everything, and you've got to do the same now. Don't wait for something to happen which will put you on the back foot. Why don't you approach him?"

Flo raised an eyebrow. "Because of Grandad's will,

remember?" After having told Rob about it, it had been easier to confide her problems to Maddy and Amber.

"How could I forget? But you can't live in fear of him turning up here one day. Figure out where you stand, legally speaking, and then make contact."

"Thank goodness for your analytical mind. You're right. Of course you're right."

"And start with the deeds to the house."

"The family lawyer retired last year and Miss Perfect is now my family lawyer."

"Miss Perfect?"

"Charlotte Kincaid."

"Oh, Charlotte. She's a lovely woman, *and* clever. She'll help you out, I'm sure. Go to her and find out for sure who owns the house and what your options are."

Flo sighed and let her head drop back as she stared at the ceiling. "You're right. Trouble is, Charlotte is also chairperson of the Festival of Lights, the person who has warned me they'll move the meetings to the community center unless I get the dining room up to scratch." She twisted around to face Maddy. "We are not, to put it mildly, the best of friends."

Maddy frowned. "But isn't Charlotte a friend of Rob's? Maybe he could put in a good word." Flo turned away too sharply for Maddy's quick mind. "Oh, Flo, she's only a friend, I'm sure of it."

"Then why are they always going off together for secret meetings?"

Maddy shrugged. "For business meetings, which have to be secret, I guess. I'd take him at his word on that one. There *are* such things as secret meetings which are purely business and don't involve anything…" She paused as she groped for the right word. She shrugged. "Personal."

"Yeah, well, it's not just that. We just don't gel, Charlotte and I."

"I've met her a few times, she's really nice, she—"

"Okay. Maybe we just got off on the wrong foot. And I do need to check out my legal position."

"So you'll have a secret business meeting?" Maddy raised a teasing eyebrow.

"Sure. You're right. If my father ever returns to make a claim on the house, I need to be prepared." Flo rose. "But as he hasn't been seen around Akaroa for over twenty years, hasn't even tried to contact me, I'm not holding my breath."

Maddy pursed her lips in concentration as she picked up her phone once more. She held it up triumphantly. "Looks like your dad hasn't put any security settings in place. And his profile and all his photos are available for anyone to see." She pursed her lips. "For even his daughter to see." She picked up her bags. "I'll go now and I'll leave my phone with you so you can have a good look through by yourself. I'll see you in about an hour, okay?"

But Flo didn't say anything. Maddy gave Flo's shoulder an awkward pat and turned away. Flo didn't even hear Maddy close the front door, or her car drive off down the street. Because all of Flo's brain and heart and gut were focused on a photo of her father. Not his profile picture, but one which had been posted recently, with the unmistakable backdrop of the Southern Alps, which ran like a backbone down New Zealand's South Island. But it wasn't this proof that he was in New Zealand which had so shocked Flo. It was the fact that she could see his face clearly, and she recognized it. It was the same face she'd glimpsed from her back porch, lit by the street lamp. The face of the strange man who'd been looking at her house *and* her, before he'd walked on.

Her father had been here, looking at her and the house, and she hadn't even known who he was. But, worse than that, he hadn't made contact with her. And that could only mean one thing. He wasn't interested in her, only what she had—the house.

FLO DIDN'T WASTE any time. The next day she dressed in her most professional outfit—black jeans and a white shirt and a blazer she'd picked up from a charity shop—and went into the lawyer's office just off the main street in a trendy brick villa which had been stripped down and made super cool. Of course it had, thought Flo, bleakly, just like its owner.

The receptionist was a young man, which didn't surprise her. Charlotte Kincaid was too much of a force to be reckoned with to have anything as stereotypical as a female receptionist. The twenty-something was sharply dressed and answered phones, operating the computer with ease, as he studied files on his desk. Of course, not just a receptionist, but some kind of law clerk, Flo surmised.

"Can I?" Flo mimed going through to what she deemed to be Charlotte's office. But the man didn't appear to hear. She shrugged but stopped short when she glanced out to a side balcony where two people stood talking. It only took her a moment to see that one of them was Charlotte, and the other was Rob Connelly. Charlotte laughed and touched Rob lightly on the arm. Flo felt sick. But Rob moved away and she could hear him making winding up sounds before he emerged into the waiting room, Charlotte having retreated into her office.

"Flo!" he said warmly, as if he hadn't been caught fraternizing with the enemy. "I didn't expect to see you here," he said with a wide grin.

"I'm sure," Flo said tightly.

His smile faded at her cool response. "Everything okay?"

He glanced back at Charlotte's office. "Are you here to see Charlotte?"

She nodded. "Business."

He grunted in surprise and shuffled his feet, suddenly unsure. "Right. I'll see you later, then, yes?"

"Sure." She racked her brain for something more reassuring to say, but couldn't bring herself to, not with the image of Miss Perfect touching Rob's arm. She felt, quite irrationally she knew, that *she* should be the only one to touch his arm. No one else. Especially no one as beautiful as Charlotte Kincaid.

"Right," said Rob, who, after glancing at the receptionist and Charlotte's closed door, pursed his lips as if determined not to say what was on his mind, and left the office. Flo watched him leave with contradictory feelings. She hated feeling jealous, but couldn't rid herself of the notion that she had cause to be.

"You can go through now," the young man said, with a smile which didn't reach his eyes and which made her feel even smaller than she felt already.

She shouldn't have felt nervous, but all of this formality was a million miles outside her comfort zone, and she found herself checking her jacket and running her tongue over her teeth to make sure there was nothing left of the last-minute muffin she'd eaten to give herself courage.

She hesitated, knocked on the door, and it swung open wide. Charlotte Kincaid stepped forward and thrust her hand in Flo's, giving it a handshake which made Flo thankful that she didn't suffer from arthritis.

"Good to see you again, Flo."

"Charlotte," Flo forced herself to say, although she always thought of her as Miss Perfect.

"Please come in. I don't think you've ever been in my office before, have you?"

"No. I try to avoid lawyers if I can." Then Flo suddenly thought that might have sounded rude. "Not that there's anything wrong with you. You're just expensive and usually mean trouble. Oh! That didn't come out right either."

Charlotte laughed. "You're correct on both counts. But hopefully, we lawyers usually fix more trouble than we cause. Take a seat and tell me what the issue is here."

Flo did just that, perching on the edge of the minimal-looking leather chair, which didn't look built for someone of normal size.

"It's the house. My family has always lived in it since it was built by my great-great-great-grandfather."

Charlotte gave a low whistle. "That's a lot of greats." She smiled, as if encouraging Flo to warm to her. But Flo couldn't.

"Yes, it is. And all those greats are like reinforcements to the ties which bind me to the house." She took a deep breath and sighed. "What I mean to say is that my house is my life. It's who I am."

Charlotte nodded. "I've always sensed that about you. Always envied you that feeling of belonging." Flo wasn't sure if she was more shocked that Charlotte had sensed anything about her whatsoever, or that she envied Flo anything. She mustn't have been able to conceal her surprise, because Charlotte suddenly looked embarrassed. "Please continue."

"But, while I understood the legal side was sorted about my owning the place, I'm not sure whether that could be challenged."

"Who would want to challenge it?"

Flo licked her lips. "My father."

Charlotte raised two perfectly formed eyebrows. "Your father." She looked down and flicked through some documents which Flo hadn't brought, but which must have been on her files. "I don't see any mention of him anywhere."

Flo cleared her throat. She seldom spoke of her father and found it difficult. "My parents married young, had me and then left to travel the world. As far as I know, my grandparents never saw, nor heard from them again."

Charlotte nodded, a cool professional nod which didn't give away her thoughts. But Flo could easily guess them.

Charlotte closed the files, rested her arms on the desk and leaned over to Flo. Flo hated the look of sympathy she thought she saw there. She guessed Charlotte had never had occasion to feel deserted by anyone, never in any doubt that she would be rich and successful and always get what she wanted.

"And you've heard from him?"

"Not directly. But we—Maddy and I—found him on Facebook. And it looks like he's living in Christchurch."

"Okay. You've done well to come to me first. I will look into the matter to see if there's anything in the old records to suggest that your father could make a claim on the house. Unless I find anything which would make a court hear your father's request favorably, I doubt he'd have a leg to stand on. But"—she clasped her hands in a professional way—"let's not get ahead of ourselves. Do you have any documentation at home that might be pertinent to the matter?"

Flo thought of the documents in her grandfather's safe, but found herself shaking her head. There was a copy, she knew, but maybe it had been destroyed and she possessed the only copy. But as soon as she denied their presence she felt a stab of guilt. What had it come to when she could tell a lie? She, Flo Pelletier, never told lies. But then, her entire world was at stake.

"No," she said firmly. "But, of course," she said, rising from her chair, sensing the ten minutes which was all she could afford was over, "I'll let you know if I find anything."

"Good." Charlotte also stood up and extended her hand to

Flo. Flo braced herself for another hearty handshake. But this one was slightly less aggressive, as if something had softened the uber-glossy Charlotte a little. "I don't want to raise your hopes, Flo but, honestly, unless we find something, I doubt you have anything to worry about."

Flo heaved a sigh of relief, hoping beyond hope Charlotte wouldn't stumble upon the one document which could ruin her life. "Thank you," she said, with a genuine smile.

"No problem. And, if there's anything else, anything at all, which you think might be pertinent to the case, just email it to me." She must have seen Flo's expression. "Or drop it in."

"I will."

With a feeling of relief, Flo thanked the receptionist and stepped outside the office. As soon as she turned around, she saw Rob, waiting for her, sitting on the post at the end of the courtyard.

"Hey there," he said, rising to his feet. "You didn't take long."

"That's good for you then, I guess," said Flo, quickly gauging the situation. "I guess you're waiting to go back inside?" She could hear the prickly edge to her voice.

"Nope." He rolled on the balls of his feet, his hands thrust into his trouser pockets as he looked down at her in a steady, frustrating way.

"What are you doing, then?"

"I'm waiting for you. Is that so hard to imagine?"

"Frankly, yes." She walked on past Rob, but he quickly fell into step beside her. Silently she cursed her short legs, which made out-walking Rob nigh on impossible.

"I don't know why it's hard to imagine. You know I like you." He placed his hand on her arm just after they'd crossed the road and stood on the seafront. "More than like, Flo. You know it. I don't know why you keep ignoring it."

"Maybe because I keep seeing you with other women?"

He frowned, as if genuinely confused. "Who?"

Flo nodded to the building from which they'd just come. "Miss Charlotte Kincaid for one."

He shrugged. "For another?"

She was getting annoyed now. "There is no other. Just Charlotte. There doesn't need to be another with Charlotte. She's more than one."

"What the hell are you talking about?"

"You know exactly what I mean."

"I don't. How can one woman be more than one?"

"When she's someone like Charlotte."

"You're jealous," he said with a grin. "That's good. I like that."

"Why do you like that?"

"Because it means you feel something for me."

"I guess lots of people have feelings for you. Like Miss Charlotte Kinkaid."

"Why do you keep coming back to Charlotte?"

"Because you like her."

"Of course I like Charlotte. She's a very nice woman."

Flo crossed her arms. "And she's attractive."

He shrugged. "Yes, I guess."

"So you like her and think she's attractive?"

"Yes, I've said so, haven't I?"

People cast glances at them as they raised their voices.

"She seems pretty keen on you."

"Does she? I hadn't noticed. I doubt it. But even if she was, I wouldn't be interested."

"Give me one good reason why not."

"Because, Flo—" He raised his voice. "She's not you!"

Flo was floored. "Not me," she repeated in a small voice.

Rob took a step closer to her. "Not you," he repeated, equally softly.

"But... her eyebrows. They're so perfectly formed."

She noticed his gaze dip to her breasts, but he quickly lifted his gaze with a smile. "And you have two perfectly formed…"

She narrowed her eyes, and he smiled and shook his head, as if to say, I'm not going there. Instead, he lifted his finger and gently stroked underneath her eye. "Eyes. I have never, in my life, seen more beautiful eyes on anyone. Your eyes are exquisite. First there's the shape of them. Large and yet slightly uplifted at the corners. A hint of feline charm. Expressive. You scarcely need to speak because I can read everything you're thinking in them."

"And what am I thinking now, smart arse?"

"You're hoping I'm going to stop because you're embarrassed enough to call me a smart arse. But I'm going to disappoint you there, because I've only just begun."

Any further thoughts evaporated, and all she could do was make a strange noise in her throat as he tickled her long eyelashes with his finger.

"Long, dark lashes which shade your eyes when you try to hide your thoughts. And then, when you open your eyes wide, there's the pièce de résistance. The color."

"Just green."

"Ha! No 'just' about it. One minute they're dark as greenstone in the depth of a mountain stream."

She rolled her beautiful eyes then. But it made no difference. It seemed nothing was going to stop Rob from describing her good points at length.

"And then, the next minute, they have a golden tinge in them, like the light has struck them, highlighting the gold streaks, separating them from the blue—like sunset."

"Sunsets aren't green."

"My point exactly."

She grabbed hold of his hand. "Enough, enough, Rob. I get it. You like my eyes." She cast a quick glance around. She could see Mrs. King who lived next door to Gabe and Maddy, stopping and talking to someone else while they made less-than-covert glances their way. "Let's take this somewhere more private, where I'm not going to be the subject of gossip."

"Now you're talking." He took her hand, and they walked over to his car. "Olly is going to Rachel and Zane's after school to catch up with his cousins. So I'm all yours."

Flo's heart skipped a beat, and other parts of her body reacted, too. It wasn't what she had in mind originally, but the thought was pretty enticing now.

It took only a few minutes to be on the road, leaving the center of town behind them, before they pulled up outside Flo's house. For once, she was glad the house was empty. Rob had continued to describe all the things he appreciated about Flo's appearance and, as they hurried through the garden up to the house, his descriptions had become cheekier and more intimate. The warmth had begun in Flo's stomach, but now her whole body was aflame with desire.

They stopped on the doorstep, and she turned in his arms. His lips were upon hers and he kissed her with a tempestuous need which exactly equaled hers. There was everything she could want in this kiss—barely suppressed need, desire, appreciation, and she was *very* much aware of how much he wanted her. He muttered under his breath.

"You are the most delicious woman I've ever met, and the only woman I want."

"More than—"

He shook his head and refused to allow herself to name the object of her jealousy. He captured her lips once more, as his hands shifted down to her bottom. He only broke his kiss to say, "I don't think I've adequately described how much I love the shape of your bottom." She squealed with laughter and pushed open the door to the house, then stopped still.

Rob bumped into her and put his hands around her waist, kissing her neck passionately.

"It's you!"

"Of course it's me," said Rob. "Who do you think it—"

He broke off abruptly as he saw what she saw. A man stood before them in the entrance to the kitchen. But not just any man. Her father.

11

"*D*ad," said Flo. Even as she said the word, it sounded strange. She'd never said the word out loud before, especially not to anyone who actually might be her father.

"Floriana," he said.

"Floriana?" said Rob, turning to Flo with a frown. "Is that your real name?"

"Her mother loved flowers and so we christened her Floriana." Her father smiled. "Floriana Rose."

Flo winced. "How did you get in?"

He nodded toward the back door. "There was a young lady here who let me in. She said she was a friend of yours—Maddy, I think she said her name was."

"Maddy let you in?"

"That's right." He looked around, evidently uncomfortable. "I hope you don't mind. I just stayed here, in the hall. It didn't seem right to wander around."

"Maddy didn't tell me."

She felt Rob's hand reassuringly on the small of her back, reminding her he was there for her, giving her strength while her mind spun. "Why didn't she tell me?" she asked. She knew she sounded petulant, but it was the easiest thing to grasp hold of. Anything but accept the fact that her father was standing in front of her.

"Maybe she had her reasons for not telling you," Rob said.

She nodded and turned back to her father. Rob was right. If Maddy *had* told her, she couldn't have said whether she'd have agreed to meet him or not. But now she couldn't avoid him—couldn't avoid the conflicting feelings that seeing her father, after so long, had created. *Her father*, who could take everything she valued away from her.

She shook her head, incredulous, wondering if the apparition would vanish. Maybe he was a figment of her imagination. But then Rob stepped forward and extended his hand to her father.

"Pleased to meet you, Mr. Pelletier," said Rob, as if this was an everyday occurrence.

Her father smiled, and Flo recognized the smile. She'd seen enough photographs of herself to know that they shared the same smile. It was like a kick in the guts to suddenly discover something she should have known growing up.

"You must be one of Jim's boys," her father said.

"Yep, Rob Connelly."

"You look like your dad. I knew him well when I was around your age. How are the rest of the family?"

"Mum and Jonny aren't with us any longer."

"Sorry to hear that. Must have hit Jim hard. Must have hit you *all* hard."

"Yep," said Rob, looking back at Flo. "Sure did."

She shook her head in disbelief that such a normal conversation should go on while the unthinkable had happened.

"What—" She had to clear her voice, which sounded hoarse and emotional. "What are you doing here?"

"I've come to see you."

"Why now?"

"Maybe because it's been too long, and it's taken me too long to realize it."

It was too much for Flo and she made a strange sound and walked into the kitchen, automatically picking up the kettle. Tears threatened, and she hadn't a clue what to say to this stranger who was her father, apart from why, why, why?

She could hear her father and Rob continue talking. Flo finished filling the kettle and banged it down on its stand. How could her father just stand in her hall and make small talk with Rob about families?

"So," she heard her father say, "Jim said you've recently returned from England."

"Yes," Rob said, before pausing and glancing at Flo. He glanced back at her father, obviously not encouraged by her expression. "I was there for nearly ten years. I'm glad to be back."

"And your brothers and sisters?"

"We're all good, thanks. Max and his wife live in Queenstown. They run a ski resort there. Lizzi is married and living in Shelter Springs."

Flo wondered if Rob was going to give her father a rundown on every member of his large family.

"Then there's Rachel, who returned to Akaroa a few years ago and lives over on the marae with Zane. Gabe is Akaroa's doctor and is married to Maddy."

Yep, it sure sounded as if Rob felt deeply uncomfortable and was determined there wouldn't be any lull in the conversation.

"And Amber lives locally with her family." Rob cleared his throat and their eyes met through the open doorway. Silence fell like a heavy weight, squashing any more thought of small talk.

Flo wandered over to the door and looked from one to the other of them. "You've missed out Cam. But, as we don't even know where he is, we'll spare my father that, shall we?" She turned to her father. "Well, you're here now. Would you like something to eat and drink?"

"I would. Thank you."

"How do you like your tea?"

"As it comes."

Why did her father's response irritate her so much? *As it comes*. It felt slippery, as if life weren't something to be grasped and enjoyed, but glided along, too lightly, without opinion. "Sugar, no sugar? Milk, no milk? Lemon, no lemon? Earl Grey, gumboot?" She raised her hands helplessly. "I have nothing to go on. I have no idea." She could feel her emotions threatening to break through. She turned away quickly and opened the larder.

"I'm sorry if I've made you angry, Floriana," said her father. "That wasn't my intention."

She gripped the larder door and turned to him. "Then what was your intention?"

"Just to see you."

"Well, you've done that. Mission accomplished. Now what are you going to do? Go away for another twenty years?"

"I guess I deserve that."

"And more," said Flo, looking around the well-stocked larder. She grunted with annoyance. "I'm out of lemons."

"I don't need lemon."

Flo shot a fierce look at her father and went out the back door to the lemon tree. The door was ajar and she could hear her father talking to Rob.

"Is she always this prickly?" her father asked.

"No," Rob said. "Only when confronted with a father who

she believes rejected her and suddenly appears out of the blue."

As Flo re-entered the kitchen, she caught sight of her father's grimace as if someone had hit him. "I deserve that. And more," he said, resting his steady green gaze on Flo.

Rob's words seemed to knock all the prickliness and defensiveness out of Flo. She sank into the nearest chair, still clutching a lemon.

"Tell me what I can do to make up for what I did," her father said.

"For what you *didn't* do," she said miserably. She lifted her face to his, again thinking it was like looking into a mirror, except his face was thin and more lined than anyone his age should be. As if he'd spent his life outside with nothing to protect himself from the elements. "All I want to know is why you and Mum wanted nothing to do with me."

"It wasn't you we were rejecting. But the whole western capitalist lifestyle."

"I was a child, for goodness' sake! Not a symbol of capitalism."

"I know. Well, I know now. But then, I guess we wanted adventure, too, and we were so young when we had you."

"Then you shouldn't have had me."

Her father had the grace to look down. "You're right, of course. It's all excuses, but if it's any consolation, our political views were pretty extreme in the early days. And then, I wasn't well and your mum kept beside me, making sure I was okay. And the longer we left it"—he shrugged—"the harder it was to think about returning. The letters your gran sent me didn't help. They told us not to bother to come back. So we didn't."

"Gran told you not to bother to return home? She never told me that!"

"She wouldn't have. She said that as far as you were

concerned, you were better off without either of us and that neither you nor she wanted to see us again. But a few months ago, I heard she died."

"Gran died two years ago."

"I heard through the grapevine. I was living in a commune in central Asia."

Flo shook her head. Her dad was as crazy as her gran had described.

"And I had to come."

"Why? To see me? Or to claim your inheritance?"

Understanding suddenly dawned on her father's face, and he tensed. "Is that why you think I've come back here? Come on," he said, walking over to her. "I'm a card-carrying communist. I've never owned anything in my life and I certainly don't intend to start now."

"Then why did you come?"

"Is it really so hard to believe I came to see my only daughter? Floriana, I don't want anything from you, nothing that you don't want to give, anyway. But I wanted to make sure you were all right. Nothing more, I promise you."

"Are you sure?" asked Rob. "Because it's some coincidence that as soon as Flo gets the lawyers involved, you come around."

"It's no coincidence. I came around a few times, trying to pluck up courage to come and see you. It was only after I received a phone call from the lawyer this afternoon telling me I had no rights to the property that I realized we definitely needed to meet. I was in Akaroa, so…" He shrugged.

Flo felt a tremor of nerves. "Why? Do you think my lawyer is lying?"

"No, I *don't* think she's lying."

"But you think *I'm* lying."

He kept his steady green gaze on her. "Are you?"

Rob exchanged a look with Flo as if to say it's time.

She knew he was right. Not because of anything her father had said, but because she couldn't cope with the deceit any longer. She jumped up, went to the cupboard and grasped the heavy ring of keys in one hand and held them up to her father silently.

"Okay, I *do* have something to show you." She heard two sets of footsteps follow her into the dining room. She fumbled a little, but eventually found the correct key and opened the safe and pulled out the papers. She turned around and held them out to her father.

"I found these recently. It seems my grandfather didn't agree with my grandmother about everything after all. He wanted you to have the house after they died."

Her father took the papers and skimmed through them. Rob came and put his arm around her and kissed the top of her head.

"You've done the right thing, love."

A double whammy. Rob approving of her actions and calling her love. She almost didn't register her father's next move. But Rob did.

"What the hell are you doing?" Rob said, starting forward. But her father was quicker and had torn the papers in half from top to bottom and tossed them into the old fire grate before Rob could stop him.

"I don't want them," said her father simply. "I loved my parents, especially my dad, and I'm grateful you've shown these papers to me. But, you know what? I knew they existed already. I'd seen them before. And I tore up that copy, too."

"I don't understand."

"Nor did your grandparents. But I only ever had one belief, and that is that no one should own anything in this world. We caretake it, and work for the good of the people, the community. Live lightly on the planet and then move on. That's all I ever wanted to do. I have a big place in my heart for this house and for you, but I would never claim owner-ship of either."

It was only then that the tears came. Later Flo couldn't have described whether they were tears of relief, or of exhaustion, or despair for what had happened in the past, or humiliation that she'd selfishly wanted something so much that she'd deny her own father it. It all mingled together in one unhappy mess and she sat down on the nearest chair, put her head in her hands and burst into tears.

They weren't pretty tears but sobs which wracked her to the core. Eventually, with Rob's arms around her as he knelt in front of her, holding her close, the sobbing subsided. When she opened her eyes and brushed away the remaining blur from her eyes, her father was still there, his green eyes watching her steadily from the other side of the room.

"I'd better go now."

"No, please stay. I've been 'prickly' as you say, *and* wrong. I was just frightened, you see. I always felt that you and Mum rejected me because I wasn't good enough for you. And Gran, while she was an amazing woman, wasn't the type of person who enjoyed discussing emotions." She glanced at Rob. Now wasn't the time to bring him in to it. But he squeezed her hand, and she knew he understood that their own break-up had done much to hurt her and make her even more protective of the little she had—her house. "Stay, and I'll show you around the house. And you can tell me about your memories of the place." He still looked uncertain. "I'd love to hear them," she pleaded softly.

Her father smiled then, and it was so warm that she felt the tears emerge once more. She brushed them away.

"I'd like that. Very much."

Little by little, as Flo showed her father around the house in which he'd grown up, she relaxed. At first she'd found it hard to settle her emotions, but with Rob's steadying presence and her father's equally laid-back presence, slowly she found her own center of calm. At the end of the tour, they found themselves in the garden.

"It's better than I remember it," said her father, looking around. "When I was a kid, I used to work in the garden. Loved nothing more than being out here." He pointed to a corner of the garden, which was one of Flo's favorites. "I created that rockery. Found the plants here-abouts and planted it all up. It looks just as I imagined it would look."

"I added the native daphne," Flo said, bending down and touching its tiny pink and white flowers. "It grows well here, and it smells so delicious."

Her father crouched down beside her. "It does. You know where I got the *Craspedia 'Kaitorete'*?" he asked, stroking the plant's soft leaves.

She shook her head. She'd always wondered. Botanists had come to her for cuttings, as it was so rare.

"I found it up in the hills."

"Where?"

"Oh—" He gestured randomly. "Some miles from here, a long way from a path or road. I always liked to go rambling. And foraging. It's how I get by—feed myself, earn some money. Do you like rambling?"

She shook her head. "Not so much. I like to be home best of all."

He nodded and stood up. He thrust his hands into the pockets of his much faded jeans. And she, once again, thought he looked too skinny, despite arms which were corded with muscles as if he'd spent a lifetime doing manual work. "You're a homebody like your gran. I prefer to be free of everything like that."

"So I guess your foraging business suits you."

He laughed. "I never thought of it as a business when I

started out. I've been foraging for food and plants for years. But it seems there's a market for it here, in New Zealand."

"So you're going to stay?" She suddenly felt anxious that he was going to disappear as suddenly as he'd come.

He considered her for a moment. "Do you want me to?"

She nodded, unable to express exactly how much she'd like that.

"Yes, I'm going to stay." He looked around, his eyes narrowing as his gaze took in the surrounding hills, bright blue sky and then turned back to her. "Yes, I reckon everything I need is here."

"Will you…"

"Will I what?"

"Will you want to move back here, into my house?"

He smiled and shook his head. "No. It's too full of memories, not all of which are good. This is your home now. Not mine. I'm happy where I am."

"Can I visit you?"

His smile broadened. "I'd like that. Very much. But don't expect a lot. I live in an old cottage with a corrugated iron shed, and what little furniture I have are things other people considered to be rubbish."

"I enjoy making things out of other people's cast-offs, too. It seems such a waste, doesn't it?"

"It's criminal. And I can see you've put the effort in with your house. But…" He glanced up at the spouting and guttering, which needed replacing, as did the roof. "You're going to need some cash to keep this place weather proof."

"Don't I know it. Rob's helping me out." She glanced at Rob, who'd taken a seat on the verandah and was pretending to read an old magazine. It wasn't one he was interested in, and she knew he was just giving them some space. "But it doesn't feel right, you know? I want to be independent. I don't want to be beholden to a man."

"Not even your father?"

She frowned and shook her head in confusion. "What do you mean?"

"Before your grandfather died, he contacted me and told me he'd left me some money."

"Really? Oh my goodness! I bet Gran didn't know about that!"

"I bet she didn't."

"Good old Grandad. I'm glad he did, though. He wanted you to be safe. To be looked after."

"And I was. Your mum made sure of that." He frowned suddenly, and toed a wormhole in the grass, flattening it before he continued to speak. He cleared his throat. "I was pretty devastated when she passed. It was very sudden. We'd argued—we never argued—and she said she was going to use some of the money to return to Akaroa to see you."

She opened her eyes wide. "She was going to come to me?"

"She was. And she would have if the bus hadn't lost its grip on the road. We were in India—Andhra Pradesh—and it was monsoon season," he said bleakly. "She was killed outright. At least I'm thankful she didn't suffer. But I'll never forget the last time I saw her was when she was walking away from me after an argument."

For the first time since he'd arrived, Flo reached out and touched his arm. He stilled and turned to her suddenly. She was closer now than she'd been before and could see tears pooling in his eyes.

"I loved your mum, Floriana. I'd have done anything for her, but she went to her grave not knowing that."

"I'm sure she knew that, Dad. You lived together for years." She glanced at Rob. "You don't always have to say the words to understand what a person feels."

"You're as wise as your gran, but with Grandad's kindness," said her father, sweeping a lock of Flo's hair off her face. "I'm glad you've got Rob."

"I'm not sure I have," said Flo.

"Come on, the man obviously adores you. And you love him, don't you?"

"Yes, I love him enough not to be with him."

Her father's face creased with concern. "What do you mean?"

"To Rob, family is everything. He wants a big family like he grew up in." She gave a slight, soft grunt of amusement verging on dismay. "He says he wants one more child than his parents had."

Her father gave a low whistle. "And that's what?"

"He wants nine children."

"And you don't?"

"It's not that. It's…" She trailed off, wondering how she'd so nearly told this man, this stranger, her father, something she'd never told a living soul. Only her doctor. Only Gabe Connelly. She shook her head. "It doesn't matter." She sucked in a deep breath and sighed. "What matters is that I've found my dad at last."

"I'm so happy," he said. He tapped his chest. "I feel at peace, more than I've felt in a long time."

"Me, too. Let's stay in touch, yes?"

"I'd like that."

"And if there's anything I can do for you, anything at all, just let me know and I'll be there for you."

He smiled. "I'd rather hoped there was something I could do for you."

It was her turn to smile. This was her father—who trod lightly on the world. "Like what?"

"Like give you the money to get this place sorted."

"That's very kind, but it will take a lot."

"As it happens, I have a lot. Your grandad gave me stocks

and shares, things which probably didn't seem to amount to much at the time. But I've had them valued and they'll be more than enough to get this house straight."

Flo pressed her hand against her stomach, unable to believe her father was saying such things. "But, but, I couldn't possibly take it. It's yours. Grandad wanted you to have it so you'd always be safe."

"I don't need money to make me safe. The only reason I kept it was to give to you one day. And, besides, your grandad's getting his wish. I have *you* now and knowing you're here makes me feel safe—in here." He tapped his heart. "And that's all that matters."

Flo could feel the tears trickle down her face. Her father reached out for her and pulled her into his embrace. "It's okay, Floriana."

"Flo, call me Flo."

"It's all going to be okay, Flo." And for the first time in her life, Flo thought that it just might be.

Rob jumped up when he saw Flo burst into tears. He was about to go over to them when he saw Flo's father gather Flo in his arms. It seemed strange for Rob to see someone else, other than him, give Flo comfort, but he forced himself to sit down again.

It had taken all his self-control to leave Flo and her father together, but he knew it was important for them both to sort this out on their own.

After a few moments, he watched them part, say a few words, and Flo's father step away. Her father looked up at Rob, waved, and went out the front gate and walked down the road. Belatedly, Rob realized that Flo's father probably had come by bus from Christchurch, or had hitch-hiked. He was certainly a man of principle. He led his life according to his principles and didn't compromise. Trouble was, it didn't make for an easy life. Not for him and not for his daughter.

Flo walked over to Rob and his heart nearly broke at the look of vulnerability in her eyes. But that vulnerability was equalled only by the width of her smile.

"He didn't leave me because he didn't want me, did he, Rob?"

Rob shook his head. "No, I reckon he went in search of something he couldn't find here. A freedom which your mum obviously cherished, too. Besides, it sounded like he had it rough mentally, and she had no choice but to be with him."

"Yes. Until the months turned into years and it became too late to return. My gran refused to see him."

"I guess she thought it was best for you."

"I know she did. She was a tough woman, but she loved me. I know that."

Hand-in-hand, they stepped into the hallway, and slowly he turned her in his arms and kissed her. "Now, I remember being in this position some hours earlier. Can you recall what we were about to do?"

"Um, I think I can."

"So, maybe we should take up where we left off?"

"Maybe we should."

And they did.

12

The weeks leading up to the Festival of Lights had sped by. Between work, getting to know her father during his visits to Akaroa, and spending every night with Rob, before he returned early to be at Belendroit for Olly, Flo hadn't had a moment to herself. Which, she considered on the morning of the Festival itself, was just as well. But, now, with Rob returned to Belendroit, and a whole fifteen minutes before she had to rise and begin catering for her house of guests, she could no longer avoid facing up to what she had to do.

She couldn't keep the secret any longer. It ate away at the heart of her and would devastate Rob. Everything was falling into place. First Rob, then her father. But the pieces still didn't come together to form a pretty picture. There was a gaping hole in the image of which only she was aware. She should have told him earlier, when they'd both awoken, in those first sweet moments as they lay in each other's arms, with nothing but the sound of the sea outside the window and the sense of endless possibilities before them. Except they weren't endless, were they? She couldn't give him what he wanted, and he needed to know. But when should she tell him?

Both of them had a busy week planned. Akaroa was full of visitors, which not only meant Amber's café needed constant supplies of baking, but it also meant the Backpackers was fully booked. It seemed everyone needed feeding, entertaining, and accommodating. Which meant she didn't have a moment to herself.

The festival opened that evening on the Akaroa Domain, where everyone would gather to finally see what lay beneath the strangely shaped features which had been under wraps for weeks. At dusk, the lights would be turned on, the mysterious features would be lit up, and the picturesque harborside town would be transformed into a place of magic. An evening of live music would follow. Daytime and evening events and activities were scheduled over the following weeks for people of all ages.

It was going to be a busy time for Flo, but that was exactly how she liked it—her house full of people and life. And now, it had the added dimension of seeing Rob each night. It should have been perfect, except for the one thing she could no longer ignore. He believed her to be the perfect woman for him, but she wasn't. He believed together they could lead the kind of life he'd always imagined for himself. He was wrong. And she could no longer delay telling him.

She'd have to tell him tonight.

FLO LEFT Etta in charge of checking in the late guests and keeping an eye on the place during the festivities. For a sixteen-year-old, the girl was certainly capable. Flo doubted if any of her guests would get away with anything under Etta's watchful eye. Etta and her mates were happy to watch the fireworks from the house, which left Flo free to go in search of Rob on the domain.

It was, predictably, crowded, and it took a little while to locate the Connellys. But, when she found Amber, Maddy, and the rest of them, there was no Rob.

"He's busy," said Amber. "Or, at least, that's what he told me."

"What can he be busy about? Everything has been done." She pointed at the different installations, now uncovered, but still unlit—their unusual shapes eerie in the slowly gathering twilight.

Amber shrugged. "You know Rob. He's never one to let the grass grow under his feet. He's off doing something or other."

Flo relaxed. Of course he was. If the past few weeks had shown her nothing else, it had proved to her he loved her and, if he wasn't here, there would be a good reason why he wasn't. "Yeah, he will be."

Gabe returned from the refreshment tent with a bottle of wine, and they sat at one of the picnic tables close to the rest of the Connellys. She jumped up when she saw her father and waved. He waved back and came and joined them. He placed his own homemade alcohol-free wine on the table. They'd have hugged except there was no room but, instead, she grinned, the sort of silly grin which she knew revealed the love which was quietly growing for her father. It was good to have someone who truly belonged to her here for a change. He smiled back and reached over the table, taking her hand in his and squeezing it and, in that moment, something settled in her heart.

She almost didn't notice the commotion around the temporary wooden dais which had been erected. Charlotte stepped up and spoke into a microphone. Flo sat back in her chair and listened to Charlotte's speech without any of her previous feelings of jealousy. Amber had been right. Charlotte *was* a nice person. Even the lengths she'd gone to on her behalf over the house, imagining Flo wouldn't be able to pay for her services, proved she was nice. Still perfect, though, she thought wryly. And then the lights were turned on.

There was a collective gasp as the darkness and shadows of the park, made deeper by the surrounding hills, were suddenly alight with shapes—some awe-inspiring, some elegant and yet others playful. The Connellys dispersed to inspect the different installations, leaving only herself and her father at the table.

She'd imagined walking around, checking out the displays with Rob, but he was still nowhere to be seen. She jumped up and craned her neck above the crowds, wishing she were taller.

"What's up?" her father asked, as she stood on the wooden bench to get a better view. But the lighted structures made the shadows deeper and darker between them, merging the jostling people into one amorphous dark shape. She sighed and jumped down.

She took a sip of her wine. "I haven't seen Rob all evening. He was meant to be here."

"I saw him earlier." Her father sat back as if that were all he needed to say.

"Where?"

"He was talking with that woman who spoke earlier. The lawyer woman."

"Charlotte?" The old jealousy reared its ugly head. "Charlotte Kincaid?"

"Yes, that's the one."

"Where were they?"

"Just up from the harbor." He nodded toward the old lighthouse. "He seemed a bit agitated and ran off toward the lighthouse."

What on earth? Flo jumped up, suddenly feeling a bit agitated herself, her mind shifting into overdrive, as she tried to make sense of why Rob would run off after talking with Charlotte. Different scenarios shot straight in and out of her mind, leaving only one. And it wasn't one she liked. She knocked back the rest of her wine and picked up her bag.

"Sorry, Dad, I have to go."

"Where are you going?" her father asked. "The festival used to go on until midnight in my day. The music hasn't even started yet."

"Yeah, I know. But I have to go home." She re-did her hair in a tight ponytail. "I have guests returning soon."

"But you have Etta there. She'll cope. I thought you had the night off."

"I do. I mean, I had. The night's over now and I best go."

Her father got up. "Let me walk you home."

"No need. You stay here and enjoy the festival and Jim's stories. You know the Connellys love having you around not least because Jim can tell you all his old stories which they've heard over and over. And you know there's always a bed for you at the house. You don't have to go back to Christchurch tonight."

"I appreciate it, Flo. And I appreciate all the work you and Rob have done to convert the sleepout for me."

She forgot her agitation for a minute and hugged her father. He was so undemanding and refused to take up her offer of a permanent room, arguing that she'd lose income. It was true, but she didn't mind. So they'd come to a compromise about which her father seemed ecstatic. The room off the garage that opened out into the garden had been converted into a bedsit for him, and he could come and go whenever he liked. He was in the midst of the garden he'd helped create, and which he loved, probably more than the house.

"It's been our pleasure, Dad. Having you in my life has been wonderful. I never thought it would happen."

He sighed. "And that's my mistake and one I'll have to live with. I'll be making it up to you for the rest of my life."

"Just promise me this."

"Anything."

"That you make it a long life."

He grinned, and his lined, leathery face formed the warm smile she'd come to know and love. Whatever his mistakes, he was a man of genuine beliefs, even if they took him too far sometimes. She kissed him on the cheek.

"Enjoy the rest of the evening."

"I'll see you in the morning, then."

"I'll have a coffee—black and hot, just as you like it— ready for you."

"Love you, Flo," she heard as she walked away.

She turned and took a few steps backwards and blew him a kiss. "Love you, too, Dad."

She welled up and had to swallow a lump as she wove her way through the crowds, heading toward the beach and then home. How her life had changed in a few short weeks. She could never have imagined a scene like this before. She felt complete. But then there was Rob. Equally, she could never have imagined re-igniting her relationship with Rob.

She was alone on the short walk along the beach, the shouts and laughter and then the music slowly receding as she moved further away from it. Every now and then, she'd stop and look up towards the lighthouse where Rob had last been seen.

Where are you, Rob? What happened between you and Charlotte, which sent you running away from me? She blinked back the tears as she peered up at the lighthouse, which had been dark for so long. The sea surged on the shore and the wind ruffled the trees.

Suddenly, a full beam of light from the lighthouse burst into life and, at the same time, a roar came from the domain. The light shone on the domain for a second before scanning across the harbor to the outer point where Belendroit lay. Briefly, the two chimneys were lit before the light swung back again across the harbor and town.

For a moment, Flo thought she was seeing things. She brushed the tears from her eyes and carried on walking. The light brought back memories of when it had last been lit. When Rob and she had been young, when his mother had been alive, and when her life had seemed so full of opportunity and hope. It felt a long time ago.

Sighing, she did as she always did, and carried on. You had to keep on going, no matter what life threw at you. It was the only way. And who knew what lay ahead?

She reached the small bridge over the stream which rang alongside her house. She'd woven fairy lights over the bridge, which appeared to float over the trickling stream. She paused for a moment on the bridge, and turned to look at the sea, which ebbed and flowed, impervious to what was going on here, what was happening to the transient life of those who lived along its shore. She felt humbled by its constancy and enormity, and her troubles diminished a little.

She took a deep breath and pulled out her phone from her back pocket. Tapping it, she realized the battery had died. Maddy was right. She needed a new phone. But not for Rob, she thought. He wouldn't be far away and if she couldn't find him, she knew, deep in her heart, that he'd come to find her. Why? Because she trusted him and, she suddenly realized, because she loved him.

It was the first time she'd acknowledged her love for him. She did a mental check of herself. How did she feel? She didn't feel *less* than, she felt *more*. All uncertainty had gone. She trusted Rob, and she trusted his love. So what if he'd had a last-minute meeting with Charlotte? He'd have a good reason.

And she knew he wouldn't be far away—no one was in Akaroa. He'd turn up. And then she'd have to tell him her secret and hope that his love for her was strong enough to accept what she had to tell him.

Then the sound of the sea merged with another sound. She turned to see Rob walking towards her from the main street. He stopped a little short.

"Is anything wrong?" he asked. "I just saw your dad, and he said you'd gone home."

"Wrong?" She shrugged, still aware of the feeling of awe the sea had given her. "No." She reached out to him. "Not now you're here."

He pulled her into his arms, gave her a big hug, and then lifted her chin and kissed her tenderly. "I've missed you," he murmured.

She smiled up at him. "You wouldn't have, if you'd been with me."

He looked over at the lighthouse. "Last minute drive to get the lighthouse working." He grinned. "Everything had been done, but we couldn't get the right lenses."

"That was you?"

"Yep. It took a lot of effort, but we got there in the end."

"We?"

"It was Charlotte who drove the project, and I did the hard yards to get it right. We didn't know if we'd be able to get all the parts in time. But earlier tonight, Charlotte gave me a parcel we'd been waiting for, so I legged it up there and put the finishing touch to it. Just in time."

"Ah, I wondered where you were. Dad saw you with Charlotte."

He frowned. "Don't tell me you thought I was having a clandestine meeting with her?"

She grimaced, embarrassed to be so easily read. "Only for a few moments. And then I thought of something which stopped me."

"Care to share?"

"I thought that no, you wouldn't be doing anything untoward because you love me."

He let out a breath with a low whistle. "Wow, I never thought I'd hear you acknowledge that."

"Me neither. But in that moment when my father told me he saw you with Charlotte and I waited for the usual blast of jealousy to hit me and it didn't, I knew I trusted you again." She gripped his arms. "I *do* love you, you know, Rob. I always have, but was too scared to admit it."

"Floriana Rose Pelletier, will you marry me?"

Her heart missed a beat, and he took her hands in his.

"Will you marry me, Flo? You know I love you. I always have and I always will."

She licked her lips and hesitated, and his grip tightened on her hands.

"Flo?"

"I'm sorry, Rob, but I need to tell you something, something which might make you want to think again about asking me."

He shook his head. "There's nothing you could say that would make me retract that question. Nothing. Will you marry me?" he said, more fiercely this time.

"Rob, you must listen to me. Before you ask me again, you must describe to me the life you see ahead of you."

"One with you, obviously." He paused, as if waiting for her to speak, but she wanted to hear what he had to say without interrupting. "You and me, here in your house, living our lives with our children, close to my family." He squeezed her hands again. "Just family. It's always been about family and that's what I want for us."

She swallowed. "And that's what I can't give you."

"I don't understand."

"You've always talked of having a big family and that's just not something I can give you." She swallowed. "I can't have children. Not ever. I've had the tests. It's been confirmed."

"No children? But you've never said anything about this before."

She shrugged, blinking to hold back the tears. "I guess it's never come up."

"How long have you…" He trailed off.

"Known I was infertile? A few years now. Gabe confirmed it with tests."

"Gabe?" said Rob, incredulous. "Gabe knew about this and said nothing?"

"He wouldn't tell you. He's a doctor, for goodness' sake. There's such a thing as confidentiality."

He rubbed his eyes. "Of course. But… Are you sure?"

"Sure, I'm sure." He closed his eyes tight, and she thought she'd lost him. She tried to pull her hands from his. "I'm sorry," she half-sobbed. But his hands simply gripped hers more firmly.

"Flo, do you remember the time when we first met?"

She shook her head. Apart from not trusting herself to speak, she found it hard to identify one single moment when she'd first met Rob.

"Nor can I. You've always been a part of my life. For forever. We're like… I don't know…" He brushed her shirt. "A piece of fabric. You run down one way—"

"The warp." She cleared her throat. "It's called the warp."

"Right. And I go across the other."

"The weft." She shot him a watery smile.

"Right. And you know one can't exist without the other."

"I guess. They just fall apart."

"They're stronger together, that's for sure. Well, it's just like us. We're stronger together."

"Rob, I can't give you what you—"

He pressed his finger to her lips to stop her from saying anything further.

"And do you remember the time when we first kissed?"

Her smile widened. "Now *that* I *do* remember. How could I forget? It was my school ball." She looked around suddenly. "It was here. You walked me home, and you kissed me here." She laughed. "We've come full circle!"

He nodded and kissed her again, drawing her into his arms more closely. He kissed her cheek and spoke more softly.

"And do you remember the time when I told you I loved you and that it would be forever?"

She nodded, her cheek brushing his. "I do."

"Then marry me, because I have only one firm vision of the future, and that's being by your side. Face it, Flo, I've *been* yours for forever and I intend to *remain* yours forever. What do you say?"

"Are you sure, Rob?"

He stroked her hair and smiled. "What more do I have to say?"

"Just that you won't resent me for not bringing you the large family you always wanted."

"What you seem to be missing is that I already *have* a large family. I have my son—our son now—and brothers, sisters, nieces and nephews, more family than anyone has a right to. I have it and so, now, do you." He huffed out a sigh. "One more time. Floriana Rose Pelletier, will you do me the honor of becoming my wife?"

She tried to contain her grin, but didn't succeed. "Well, put it like that, and how could I refuse?"

He laughed, lifted her in the air and swung her around

before setting her on her feet again. He brushed the hair off her face and searched her eyes, as if he was looking deep into her soul. "I promise you, Flo, you won't regret a minute of it. You've made me the happiest man in the world and I fully intend to dedicate my life to making you the happiest woman."

"You already have," she said, before he took her hand and they ran into the house, past her guests and Etta and her friends who lingered on the back deck. They bid them a brief goodnight before Rob tugged her hand and they ran up the stairs.

As they quickly undressed by the light of the stars and the beam of the lighthouse, which periodically swept through the uncurtained window, Flo could hear Etta—her niece now, she thought—and her other guests relaxing out the back deck, could hear the sounds of the families and community who still partied to the music from the domain, and knew she'd found a place at the heart of her world with the man who would be forever hers.

EPILOGUE

Flo looked around her dining room table, happy to see all the old china she'd inherited in use for once. Newly decorated—the fresh paint smell replaced by the heavy scent of roses in the vase, the wedding feast laid out along the opened-out kauri dining table—the place looked the best it had ever looked. Olly had ended up sitting between her and Rob, but not for long. As soon as he was able, he joined his cousins outside in the garden, around which lanterns hung in memory of Rob's mother.

"Well, Mrs. Connelly, and how are you feeling?"

"Happy, Mr. Connelly," she grinned. "Very happy."

Rob's arm rested along the back of her chair. He grinned and stroked under her hair, just above the nape of her neck. She almost whimpered with pleasure. It seemed loving Robert Connelly never grew stale.

"Me, too. I think Dad has recovered from the fact you wanted our wedding reception here rather than at Belendroit."

They both looked over to where their fathers were deep in conversation.

"Come on, let's escape."

Flo didn't need asking twice. She took his hand, and they slipped outside. Tables were also placed outside on the sand and a few people held up their drinks to them as they passed by, on their way to the only remaining empty table. It was closest to the sea.

Rob looked around. "Doesn't look like people want to leave."

"And who can blame them?" Flo said. "This is the best place in the world."

He took her hand and kissed it. "Because you're here."

"Rob Connelly." She felt suddenly embarrassed. She still couldn't get used to someone saying such things to her.

"Flo," he said, shaking his head in mock exasperation. "You're just going to have to get used to me saying things like that. I've never lied and I'm never going to. I love you and I'm going to keep on telling you every day for the rest of our lives until you believe me."

She grinned as she allowed the delicious warmth of knowing she was loved to flood her veins. She sighed and looked flirtatiously into his eyes.

"In that case," she said, brushing her knuckles over his lips, "I don't think I'm ever going to tell you I believe you, because I never want you to stop saying it."

"Because you don't believe me?"

"I really can't say," she said, her grin mischievous now. "But what I can say is that I love you." She stroked his hair which the wind had ruffled. "More than life itself."

He sighed and glanced up at the house. "Then what are we doing here when there's a perfectly good bed upstairs waiting for us?"

"Good point." They rose and said goodnight to the few remaining people they passed, outside on the veranda of the house, and inside. Olly was going to spend a few days with

Rachel and Zane on the marae, something about which Olly was ecstatic, as he could hang out with his cousins Etta and Aimee. They were alone in the hallway, and paused for a moment to kiss.

They were about to go upstairs when the front door opened suddenly, and Charlotte stepped in hurriedly, glancing behind her with concern.

"What's the matter, Charlotte?" asked Rob. "Something happened?"

Charlotte looked unusually flustered. "No. Not really. I just thought I'd come back until the coast is clear."

Rob peered outside. "The coast is clear? What do you mean?"

"I mean, there's a strange man outside."

Rob and Flo exchanged grins. "Not another one."

Charlotte shot Flo a questioning look. "How many strange men do you have outside your place?"

"The other one was Dad. What does this one look like?"

"Around thirty, long hair, tall. Looked as if he'd walked a long way—dusty, unkempt looking."

Rob and Flo's gazes no longer held humor. "We've got a drifter outside? Rob, perhaps you should go check?"

"Sure." Rob began

"Anything else about him?"

Charlotte looked a long way away, and her expression suddenly changed. "And he had *the* most intense blue eyes. Actually," she said, glancing from one to the other, "he was the most handsome man I think I've ever seen."

"But he unnerved you?"

"Yes, but it wasn't how he looked which unnerved me. Well, not much. It was what he said."

Rob licked his lips. "What did he say?"

Charlotte's beautiful brows dipped into a frown. "That

was the strangest thing. He asked me if he was too late for the wedding."

Rob paled and walked outside without saying anything further.

"Where's he going?" Charlotte asked.

Flo reached out and put a calming hand on Charlotte's arm. "He's going out to see his brother, who he hasn't seen in years. The man you just described is Cameron Connelly."

AFTERWORD

Dear Reader,

I always enjoy reading and writing stories in which there is a second chance to rekindle a love which had once been all-consuming. For Rob and Flo, while time had knocked off a few rough edges, made them a little wiser, it had also made them wary. But the love was still there and, with work, they found their happy ending. They certainly deserve it.

Now, it's time to write about Miss Perfect, as Flo called her. But who is really perfect in this world? Certainly not the beautiful Charlotte Kincaid, no matter what Flo thinks. And I couldn't resist putting in a late appearance by the mysterious Cameron Connelly. Want to find out more? Read on!

Happy reading!

Sophie

YOURS TO LOVE

BOOK 6 OF LANTERN BAY—CAMERON & CHARLOTTE

Opposites attract but for how long?

Charlotte Kincaid is 'Miss Perfect'. She's a smart lawyer, works hard for the community and is drop-dead gorgeous. At least that's what everyone else sees. But, inside, Charlotte is an emotional wreck. She believes her secret is safe because no one can see past her glossy image to the real her, right?

Wrong. The elusive Cam Connelly returns (late) for his brother Rob's wedding after traveling all over the world for years, refusing to put down roots. Because who needs a home and family? Certainly not the incredibly intelligent, stubbornly principled, eco-warrior Cam. But then he meets Charlotte who intrigues him with her combination of smarts and well-hidden vulnerability.

It's Christmas at the Connellys and anything could happen— maybe even finding a love which could last forever?

ALSO BY SOPHIE HAYDON

The Mackenzies

A Place Called Home

Secrets at Parata Bay

Escape to Shelter Springs

What you See in the Stars

Second Chance at Whisper Creek

Summer at the Lakehouse Café

Lantern Bay

Yours to Give

Yours to Treasure

Yours to Cherish

Yours to Keep

Yours Forever

Yours to Love